Encore

The Third Anthology

of the

Lake Writers

A Project of the Lake Writers

The Literary Branch
of
Smith Mountain Arts Council

Published by
Snowy Day Publications
Hardy, Virginia
www.snowydaypublications@gmail.com

ISBN: 9781795059817

Cover photo by Tom Howell

www.smithmountainartscouncil.com

Introduction

Since it was established in 2000 as an arm of The Smith Mountain Arts Council, the Lake Writers group has carried out its mission of furthering the art of writing in the three counties surrounding Smith Mountain Lake.

The group meets twice a month. On each second Friday of the month we meet at the SML/Moneta Library, and on each fourth Friday of the month at the SML Association office.

Membership and meeting attendance is open to all who share the desire of furthering the art of writing. Most of our members are published authors and offer support and guidance from the first draft to published work.

In 2013 our first anthology, *Voices from Smith Mountain Lake,* was published, followed by a second anthology, *Reflections on Smith Mountain Lake,* in 2016. A satirical work, *Nekkid Came the Swimmer,* was published in 2015.

Active members of the Lake Writers have individually published more than nine novels, mysteries, books of poems, and short story collections during the 2017-2018 time period. Several writers have successfully completed their first published works. Since the founding of the group, members of the Lake Writers have published over 100 books.

The third anthology you hold in your hands is the work of many of these authors. It is a work to commemorate the 30th anniversary of The Smith Mountain Arts Council and its mission.

Special thanks to the committee that selected the pieces to go into the anthology—Betsy Ashton, Judy Helms, and Linda Kay Simmons; to editors Jim Morrison and Larry Helms; to Tom Howell for his work on the cover; and to Chuck Lumpkin for preparing the manuscript for publishing and for overseeing its publication.

We hope that you enjoy this anthology and that you will join us for the Arts Council's next 30 years.

Mark Young
President, Lake Writers
2016-2018

Contents

Poetry

Raising Ben

BETSY ASHTON

hold my hand
don't let go
I'll help you walk

time to eat
it's your favorite
I'll feed you

give me a sign
a smile something
show me you know I'm here

speak
one word any word
let me hear your voice

Mama

No, not Mama
just me Kathy
your daughter

Nonfiction

Looking Forward

PEGGY CLUTZ

The dining room is beautiful with colorful carpeting and upholstery on the chairs all illuminated by several large brass chandeliers, and lovely dinner music from the 1930s and 1940s fills the room. Diners sit at assigned tables and beware the person who sits in the wrong chair. Since there is no chatter in this room, you hear only the scraping of silverware against plates and the clink of spoons in sweet tea glasses. For this experience, they all lined up 30 minutes before mealtime.

I am a visitor at my Mom's table of contemporaries, people known as the greatest generation. I ache when I think that 50 years ago these people had busy lives raising children, going to work and war, making important decisions regarding their present and future lives, and looking forward to their retirement. Now the seasons pass by their windows as they sit in their rooms, nodding off in the glow of the TV until the next highlight of their day—another meal or bedtime.

I'm not sure I want to look too far forward without a tissue in hand.

Nonfiction

The Taxi Ride

PEGGY CLUTZ

The idea I didn't use swirled around for a few days and found its way into a taxi cab in Manhattan, where it landed lightly amongst the volumes of papers the cabbie had stashed on the front passenger seat—his filing cabinet, he called it. It sat there for months, quickly getting covered over by more slips of paper, almost being smothered, until the cabbie picked up a fare outside of the Algonquin and the idea started shivering with excitement. The cabbie didn't even notice the quivering stack of papers as his fare climbed into the back seat. Or that two pieces of paper (with the idea sandwiched between) had been blown under the front passenger seat and were resting comfortably against the newly-seated passenger's left foot, almost hugging it.

Hoping to get a bigger tip, the cabbie started chatting up the customer, Mr. C, who seemed more interested in staring blankly out the window than conversing. Deep in thought, Mr. C had a big decision to make, and he could let nothing distract him. The vibration coming from the cell phone in the inside pocket of his suit coat startled Mr. C back to reality. After listening to the message, he threw a twenty-dollar bill at the cabbie—for maybe a five-dollar fare—and quickly exited the cab, stumbling as he ran toward the nearest building, firmly placing his back against the wall for support. Seeing his ashen face, a few brave New Yorkers stopped to ask if he was OK. He started crying and screaming that he didn't have to make the decision after all, it must have been made for him by a higher power.

Meanwhile, the idea once again floated around, waiting to be of use to someone who needed it for peace. Ideas should always be used for peace, shouldn't they?

Nonfiction

Our First Summer at Smith Mountain Lake

SUSAN CORYELL

We bought our lake cottage in 1990, eleven years before we retired to the lake. On the water with a large dock, it was the perfect get-away from chaotic Northern Virginia where we lived and worked.

Since I taught, my summers were free, so our two pre-teen kids, the dog, and I spent every day from June to September at Smith Mountain Lake. Husband Ned made it to the cottage most weekends, usually accompanied by a car full of our children's friends who would stay the week and then trek back to NOVA the following weekend. They played and sang and boated and skied from dawn to dark, causing our new neighbors to dub ours "The Loud Dock." It looked like a continual yard sale going on.

Lots of memories, many of which required a sense of humor and the ability to laugh at our own constantly-challenged sense of perspective.

We acquired a big Zodiak blowup boat we called "Sled" and attached a 3.5 horsepower motor to the back. The kids spent hours chugging around our cove, dragging their friends on a knee board or puttering out to the islands nearby to beach the boat and explore.

Once Ned took out the big rubber raft to fish. A lake policeman hailed him and asked for the registration. "It's just an oversized inner tube. Why do I need a registration?" Ned asked.

"If it has a motor, it requires registration, sir."

After paying the ticket, Ned went to register Sled. "Where do you keep the boat when not in use?" was one question on the form. "In the trunk of my car," Ned wrote, feeling vindicated at long last.

I vividly remember my first encounter with a local produce stand owner. Though the corn looked gorgeous and fresh, my urban skepticism caused me to question, "And, when was this corn picked?" In NOVA, "fresh" produce was often days old by the time it arrived at the market.

The old chaw-bacca took his time, deliberately rolling up his sleeve and peering for a while at his watch. "'Bout twenty minutes ago," he drawled.

I looked up then and realized the corn field was right behind him in his own back yard. I never asked that question again.

Ned and I stayed in touch via cell phone during the week. One sunset evening as I sat on the deck enjoying the water view, he called. We talked a while and then I asked, "What in the world is all that noise in the background?"

"Oh, I'm driving Route 66. It's the traffic," Ned said.

After more conversation, he asked me, "What's the racket I hear in your background?"

I felt a bit guilty when I answered, "It's the birds."

"Wanna trade places?" Ned asked.

Nonfiction

I'm a Lump

SUSAN CORYELL

Okay, I admit it. I'm a LUMP. That's an acronym for Lost, Unidentified, Misguided Person. Actually my whole family suffers from this malady. We laugh about being LUMPs and regale one another with recent horror tales at family reunions, but it's really rather embarrassing at times and *always* inconvenient. You see, although we are, on the whole, a well-educated and intelligent lot, not a one of us has what you'd call a sense of direction. We cannot read maps, tell east from west, or even turn left at the third light without a great deal of angst.

My brother John, for example, has a PhD, speaks three languages, and has published two large, scholarly books, but his wife Jean has to direct him home from the grocery store, especially if it's raining. The last time John and Jean visited us in Northern Virginia, we went to dinner at the Chesapeake Bay Seafood Restaurant. John got lost while returning to our table to leave a tip. We found him fifteen minutes later bobbing about the labyrinthine dining rooms looking for a familiar face.

Then once my sister left her Fairfax home and took Rte. 495 to Alexandria to visit a friend. When she was ready to return to Fairfax, she suddenly found herself forced into making an instantaneous decision while bumper-to-bumpering on the Beltway; she could either follow the sign to Richmond, or the one to Annapolis. Nothing on any of the signs about Fairfax, of course. "With lightning logic," she later reported, "I reasoned I'd come south to Alexandria; therefore, I must want to go north to return home—so I took the Annapolis exit and—you guessed it—crossed the Potomac River to face the Welcome to Maryland sign." What a LUMP!

And then there was the time my other brother (also a PhD) tried, unsuccessfully, for four hours, to find Q Street in Washington, D.C., for an appointment with a client from Georgia. He gave up and rescheduled the conference in Atlanta. He figured it was easier to fly to Atlanta than to drive in D.C.

Well, I've suffered the final humiliation with today's debacle. I have just returned from NOT driving the carpool to dancing lessons. Yes, that's right. NOT taking the four little ballerinas to class in Springfield. Oh—I picked them up right on time this morning in our Oakton neighborhood, and I faithfully followed the directions given by my spouse (who is most definitely NOT a LUMP). But where I took them, actually, turned out to be Rosslyn, not Springfield, and, by the time I'd got that far, we'd missed class entirely. My map-maker had neglected to tell me to turn OFF RTE 66 ONTO RTE 495 and, for a LUMP like me, that was a fatal omission.

It is humbling to have to tell the neighborhood mothers who would not dream of getting lost on the way to Springfield that we never made it to ballet lessons today. I toyed with the idea of lying about the entire incident and swearing the little ballerinas to secrecy with an ice cream bribe, or with stopping off at the Smithsonian, where I guess I would have eventually ended up, making a cultural outing of the whole mess, but I swallowed my pride and came back home via RTE 50 (I think) and told my sad tale.

Now, I've decided to organize a LUMPs Anonymous. Surely there are others like my family and me out there ready to come out of the closet. Think of the programs we could have at our meetings! Guest speakers from AAA and the Highway Department; workshops in map-reading, gas-station stopping and picnic-packing for LUMPs lost on interstate trips. Why, the possibilities are unlimited! Best of all, we'd be sure to designate alternative meeting places for all LUMPs who get lost en route to our meetings. LUMPs of the world, unite!

Nonfiction

Salute Mom

KAREN DEBORD

Come the bluebird bodily bursting
Into my windows he did bore
Flickering while fighting his own reflection
Clamoring, clamoring more and more.
Futile attempts to best the other
Mirroring bluebird reflected, he.
Then time came—he calmed his clamor.
Peace to him comes—evermore.

Did you ever experience emotions coming out in words or prose? It's my therapy, so thanks for indulging this blogger this time! The verses are true! For three days, we had a bluebird attacking his own reflection against the window. Symbolic perhaps, the same three days paralleled my mother's final decline. She had stopped swallowing in her last days while struggling to retain her dignity as she drew closure to the seven-year co-habitation with the disease of Alzheimer's. Granted, I had already mourned the passing of my strong role model and the competent woman I knew and loved as she shrank into the grasp of this horrible disease. But the legacy she left is remarkable.

Indeed, when the bird stopped, she, too, drew her last breath. On Memorial Day our family gathered to pay tribute to Mom. I couldn't have been prouder to have been a part of my family that day. The grandchildren took part in the service, as did my brother, sister, and I.

The energy of the room embodied the life that she lived, loved, and passed on to us. She served as a stellar role model, working

mother, and grandmother. It is that energy and our newfound re-
newal that we must continue to carry forward as her legacy—pro-
ductive, giving, humoring, holding, and loving. It is this legacy that
we must pass on within our family, to our children so that from
generation-to-generation we deliver with the same integrity what
we witnessed in her death. Remember who brought you into this
world. Salute Mom.

Nonfiction

Bumpin the G's

KAREN DEBORD & JACK PHILLIPS

Yes this happened—but from differing perspectives.

His story: Flying out of Raleigh, Karen and I spent the weekend in Virginia (Friday night in Roanoke, Saturday night in Richmond). We had a pretty strong headwind on Friday, averaging about 135 knots groundspeed. Saturday we had a great tailwind as we flew east to Richmond. I saw consistent groundspeeds of 198 knots (227 mph) but never could quite get it over the 200-knot mark. The whole trip (124 nm) took 40 minutes. It is at least a 3-hour drive.

Her story: We had a great time visiting friends in Richmond on a February weekend. When we fly, friends seem so much closer! The weather was clear, and it took only 45 minutes to get from Raleigh to Roanoke, then some 40 minutes from Roanoke to Richmond. We stayed at an inn near the airport since they advertised on their website that they had free shuttle from the airport. We landed at 1:00 p.m. and called for that shuttle, only to be told that it was not available. They suggested we take a cab. I reluctantly told them ok and that we would be right over to check in. To that they responded that check-in is at 3:00 and they would have to charge us an extra day stay for early check-in. I called my friends to come get us. Gee!

His story: For some reason, we had to stay at the airport a little longer until our friend arrived to pick us up. But a cool C-5A Galaxy landed, and I was able to check out the other crafts parked nearby.

Her story: When he flies, he thinks of nothing else except airplanes. I guess this is a good thing! The next morning, we had planned to stay for brunch with all our friends, but Jack said to eat fast since we better leave sooner as opposed to later. After a quick breakfast, we packed up and made our way to the airport. No shuttle was available (again!), but luckily our friends who also stayed at this upstanding inn gave us a lift!

His: When I saw the forecast, I decided the earlier we left, the better, and I'm glad we did. We took off from Richmond International (RIC) at 10:00 a.m. Surface winds for takeoff (we were using runway 20) were 250 degrees at 25 knots. Good thing an RV-4 has a pretty good rudder. Our course was 226 degrees with the winds from 260 at 59 knots, giving us a groundspeed of only 118 knots, so what should have been a 45-minute flight took an hour and 10 minutes. And that was 70 minutes of pure turbulence. It was the most uncomfortable flight I've ever made.

Her: Ditto! It was really bumpy, and I could feel the plane lifting up and down. I was even hitting my head on the canopy, and I couldn't read my book. Putting the book aside, the jolting was making me feel queasy. Flying above the clouds at 6500 feet, I was freezing even while wearing my gloves and coat.

His: There were 59-knot headwinds and surface winds that were 22 knots gusting to 31 knots. I had on the heater, and all it did was warm my right calf and foot. Good thing we got home when we did, because later the peak gusts went to 53 knots!

Her: I could smell that the heat was on but could not feel it. Jack said this flight wasn't dangerous—just bouncy and uncomfortable. He kept laughing each time we gained or lost 400-500 feet. Since we sit tandem, he could not see my face. I was not laughing. Now I was holding the barf bag trying to determine if I could avoid using it.

His: The turbulence about beat us to death, with the G meter ranging from -0.5 to + 3.1 G's.

Her: Jack kept announcing to me what "Gs" were involved. I tossed my cookies just as the Raleigh Durham International Airport (RDU) was in sight. This was not where we would land, but it was close.

His: Karen decided her breakfast would be more comfortable in a sack. Poor girl—first time she's ever gotten sick while flying with me. By the time we got back to our local Cox Field, RDU (Raleigh Durham International) was calling the surface winds 280 degrees at 21 knots with gusts to 31. Fortunately, the runway at Cox is 09/27, so I didn't have too much crosswind to worry about, but I would be landing downhill.

Her: I had my eyes closed, trying to settle my stomach.

His: I called into Cox Field to ask if there was anyone in the traffic pattern. Nobody else was.

Her: Wonder why?

Fiction

One Word

JANIS ERICKSON

Jack voluntarily stayed late at work…again. Coming home brought him no joy. His little boy didn't care. Austin's bedtime was 7:00, and the microwave clock read 7:42. Wonder what they had for dinner? He popped open the microwave and lifted the edge of the paper towel. Congealed gravy hid whatever lay beneath; probably turkey and mashed potatoes, a favorite of Austin's. He hit the reheat button and sat on the barstool.

"Hi, Jack. We missed you at dinner." The greeting lacked any warmth. Peggy had gotten used to his absences.

"Design deadline on the Cincinnati project. Sorry." Jack stood and gave his wife a kiss on the cheek. They both had their parts to play: she, the good mother, he, the provider. He knew he wasn't a good father. He had planned to be. All during the pregnancy, while the excitement of parenthood loomed, and the first year caring for Austin, their love continued to grow. They had named the baby after Peggy's father, who had been killed during the Vietnam War.

The microwave beeped. Jack set the plate on the counter. "Want to join me? Do we have any wine?"

Peggy pulled a bottle of white Zinfandel from the refrigerator and attempted a smile as she poured the wine. "Our meeting with the therapist this afternoon was good."

Peggy followed up with all the latest information about autism. The speech therapist had been recommended by a mother in the support group. Jack had gone with Peggy once, but with only one other man in the room, he felt out of place. Jack didn't care about the other children or how their parents were coping. He just wanted a son he could hug and would hug him back. Maybe even call him "Dad." Neither wish was likely to be granted. Peggy had taken charge of Austin; Jack was off the hook.

"What's the latest?"

"Well, it seems it's possible that there's a trigger to help Austin move out of his inner world and into ours. We just haven't discovered it yet. With the increase in cases, more research is being funded. Children in a new study seem to latch onto one area of interest. This interest becomes a conduit to developing verbal and tactile communication," Peggy explained, probably word-for-word what the therapist said.

"Do you have any ideas for Austin?"

"I think I do. While Austin was napping, I arranged all his toys around the family room. Later, I set him in the middle of the room and left. I peeked back in every five minutes. At first he stayed where I put him; after fifteen minutes, he circled the room slowly. He made his choice. For over two hours he only played with the set of zoo animals you brought back from your Cincinnati trip. He didn't even notice when I removed the other toys." Peggy took a deep breath and continued. "I approached him quietly and sat down without touching him, of course."

"More wine?" The touching thing got to Jack every time. Peggy had to touch Austin getting him dressed, putting him in the car seat or other basic stuff. He would stiffen his little body in response. If Jack tried to touch him, he'd go ballistic. Jack had totally backed off and only looked after Austin when Peggy went to the support group.

With an understanding glance, Peggy got on with her story. "I picked up one of the animals, a giraffe I think. I put it back down. I did the same with a hippo. When I picked up the lion, I made a growling noise. Austin reached for the lion, and he put it back. I picked up the gorilla and took a shot at my best monkey sound. Austin reached for the toy, and his hand touched mine; he didn't flinch at all! Jack, I did this with all the pieces over and over. I lost track of time. When I got up to leave, Austin followed me into the kitchen. He never does that."

"Why are the animals tossed all over the floor?" Jack wondered how the game or experiment ended.

"After dinner, I told Austin it was time for his bath and bedtime story. Instead of heading upstairs, he returned to the family room and moved the animals apart from each other purposefully. I thought I'd leave them until Austin gets up in the morning. What do you think?"

"Not sure. You're always the first to notice any changes. The fact that he followed you to the kitchen means what?"

"I was part of the game. With me gone, the game ended?"

"Do you want to watch a movie?" Jack changed the subject. Whatever hope Peggy had at the moment wouldn't last. Austin's autism—say that three times quickly—wasn't going away. Jack remembered thinking "tongue twister" when they got the diagnosis. He wanted to call Austin by his middle name, John. It had been a toss-up whether his name or Peggy's dad's name came first on the birth certificate anyway. Although he didn't really identify with John—he'd been called Jack his whole life. But Peggy wanted to stick with Austin.

"No, I want to check out a few sites on the computer."

"Guess I'll read in bed. Good night." He dutifully kissed his wife on the cheek before he left the kitchen.

***

Lunchtime at the office was hardly a scheduled event. The status of the current architectural contracts seemed to determine when, or even if, lunch would happen. Today his boss invited him to lunch. Jack did a quick mental inventory of the projects that were on his desk. He wondered what Larry wanted to discuss.

"Jack, everyone in Cincinnati is ecstatic with your renovation ideas for the African quadrant of the zoo. They'd like you to be on site during construction. We can set your family up in a furnished apartment for as long as it takes." Larry got right to the point. The waiter delivered two beers. Jack didn't usually drink at lunch, but his boss insisted. Larry reached across the table to clink bottles. "Cheers and congratulations!"

"I'll talk it over with my wife. She just found a therapist for

Austin. What time frame are we looking at?"

"Within the next thirty days. The paperwork and funding are in order. This is a big one for our company."

Jack called out a greeting. He didn't want to startle Austin. He was home early for the first time in over a week. Peggy poked her head around the arched door. "In here, Jack."

"Where's Austin?"

"That's what I want to show you."

Jack hung his jacket over the banister before following his wife into the family room. Peggy had moved the furniture around and covered the tables with some carpet remnants. Austin stood beside one of the end tables. He had a plastic monkey clutched in his tiny hand. He picked up a miniature tiger that was beside his left foot. He stood the animal beside another wildcat, then eased up to his mother and grabbed her hand. Peggy let out a soft growl before Austin let go.

"You try, Jack." Peggy whispered.

He shadowed Austin over to the folding table. Jack picked up a brown chimpanzee and a series of "eh, eh, ehs" escaped from the back of his throat. Austin reached for the toy, and Jack let it go. At three years old, Austin was about eye level with the table top. Austin placed both monkeys on the table. He quickly made a bee-line for the coffee table. He picked up the elephant and, before the count of three, positioned it back in the exact spot. Jack had barely taken two steps when the pressure of the small hand grabbing his caused a lump to form in Jack's "monkey" throat. He needed to come up with an elephant call. Jack pictured the elephants at the Cincinnati zoo trumpeting to their mates and babies. He mimicked the sound to the best of his ability. Austin went to get another zoo animal.

Peggy had him in a bear hug. "Now what do you think?"

Jack turned around. Peggy wiped the tears from his face and mirrored his smile. This had to be the breakthrough the therapist had alluded to. Jack couldn't wait to tell Peggy about a move to Cincinnati. He would take Austin to a real zoo. Maybe hearing the animals' vocalizations would jump-start Austin's speaking voice.

Jack felt a bit of the hope that was generally reserved for his wife.

***

The weather report had been for mostly cloudy skies. But as Jack and Austin pushed through the turnstile of the entrance to the children's zoo, the sun illuminated the entire area. Jack hummed the tune of the Sesame Street song...*sunny days, sweeping the clouds away.* At the elephant habitat, a baby elephant trumpeted. Austin turned towards Jack, and their world changed forever with one word.

"Daddy."

Fiction

Requests from Beyond

JANIS ERICKSON

The first time I laid eyes on a dead body was shortly after my fifteenth birthday. The room was eerily quiet as dust particles disturbed by my mop floated in the stagnant air. Mrs. Lucas didn't call out her usual greeting when I bumped the bedrail in an attempt to get the dust mop farther under her hospital bed. Jostling the bed a second time, I extracted the mop. Still no comment from the grouchy old woman who lay facing the wall; something wasn't right. I checked the clock on the bedside table. It was just after 9:30, rather late for Mrs. Lucas to be sleeping. The breakfast trays would have been collected an hour ago by Leslie. She started her shift at 7:00 a.m. I punched in at 9:00 and most Saturdays had the place clean before noon.

"Good morning, Mrs. Lucas." I waited for the usual sarcastic response. Silence. Very gently, I patted the blanket covering the motionless figure. Nothing. I walked to the head of the bed and peered at the face.

Tell my daughter to check the drawer of the desk. It has a false bottom. Now go get the nurse dear. The whisper crept into my ear coming from somewhere close behind me. The face on the pillow remained immobile. I spun around expecting to see another resident of the nursing home, but there was no one there.

I ran to the nurses' station only to find it vacant. I continued to the kitchen, where I found Leslie washing the breakfast dishes. "Do you know where Helen is?" I gasped out the question and collapsed against the counter.

"What's wrong? You look like you've seen a ghost."

I guess if you believe in that sort of thing, then maybe Leslie was right. Perhaps I had heard a ghost. I blurted out my suspicion as to the status of the resident in Room 3. "I think Mrs. Lucas is dead."

"Oh my! Helen is with Mr. Curry. I'll go get her, you sit and wait here." Leslie dried her hands on a worn towel and left the room.

"I didn't mean to frighten you. Don't forget to tell my daughter...."

I jerked my head up and glanced around. What was happening to me? There was no one else in the kitchen. I walked over to an open door leading to a small sitting room. Empty. I cut back through the kitchen and surveyed the hallway. Not a soul in sight. Now what?

Leslie returned and offered me a drink of water. "Helen has gone to check on Mrs. Lucas. She asked that you continue cleaning the other rooms if you are able. Once she knows what's what, she'll find you."

I headed up to the second floor. Since I had left all my cleaning supplies in room 3, I would need replacements from the cleaning closet. Mindlessly I grabbed another dust mop and cloth, lemon cleaner, paper towels, window cleaner...

"I know you can hear me. Please, my daughter needs to know..."

All the supplies that I held in my arms went clattering to the floor. I whipped around in a circle looking for a real person, but I was pretty sure I wouldn't see anyone. Should I reply?

It was worth a shot. I didn't even know Mrs. Lucas' daughter, yet I wouldn't want her to think I was crazy. I needed to stop the dead Mrs. Lucas from following me around; it was unnerving. If I agreed to her request would she go away? "OK, I'll tell her. Will she come here? Do I need to go to her house?" I waited for an answer, but there were no further messages from Mrs. Lucas that day or any other. Over the years one of the many things I would come to realize when dealing with the dead—I was on my own as to how best to satisfy their demands.

Fifteen...over sixty years ago now, but I can remember word -for-word my conversation with Mary Lucas Clark. Helen had called Mrs. Clark, and she arrived at the nursing home within 45 minutes. I found her sitting in a chair by the bed holding her mother's hand.

"Hello. Excuse me for disturbing you. I'm sorry about your mother." I gathered up the cleaning supplies.

"Thank you. I'm waiting for some folks to take Mother to the Farley Funeral Home downtown. Are you the girl that found her?"

"Yes, and I have a message for you." And then I told her about the desk. I let her believe my knowledge of a secret compartment came to me while her mother was still alive. It would take me a long while to admit to anyone that I was a conduit for the recently deceased.

About a week later, a major story appeared in the local town paper. The headline declared, *Hidden Treasure a Windfall for Town.* The article described the secret compartment of an antique desk where a bank book, with a substantial balance, was discovered along with written notarized instructions as to the dispersal of the funds. Scholarships in Mrs. Lucas' name were to be established at my high school, and more than a dozen charitable causes were each to receive thousands of dollars. There was a brief mention as to how the bank book came to light, but my name didn't make the paper this time. A thank-you note from Mrs. Clark, however, arrived at the nursing home. She expressed her gratitude to everyone on the staff who had cared for her mother and then mentioned she would like to take me to lunch for a chat. This piqued the curiosity of Helen and Leslie. Relationships with family members of our residents had never been encouraged, although they weren't forbidden either.

"What do you think she wants to chat about?" As the head nurse, Helen tried to stay on top of anything concerning her twenty-four patients. Well, make that twenty-three. A new resident hadn't moved into Room 3 yet.

"She probably wants to know what else I might have talked about with her mother. Maybe she thinks there is another fortune stashed away."

"I must say I'm surprised that Mrs. Lucas confided in you, Jill. Her life was a closed book to most of us."

"She didn't confide in me. Just that one thing is all." I felt uncomfortable not telling the truth to Helen. I sure needed this job, and I knew how crazy it would sound if I admitted hearing voices —or even the one voice. All these years later, I have lost track of the number of voices that have demanded to be heard. I could never tune them out for long and generally found it easier to get on with their wishes than put up with the constant pestering. I welcomed the voices that offered me advice in dealing with the newest member who had crossed over. Of course, not all these encounters had a happy ending.

Now that I am on my own deathbed, I contemplated what I might have left undone that would require my reaching out to a willing medium. Nothing that I could think of, so I counted the ceiling tiles innumerable times out of boredom; it was a struggle to refrain from doing it again. I should pay attention to what the health aide was saying. Yet, whenever I did, my impatience reached another level. I wished I could tell her to shush up, but since my third stroke any hope of gaining back my words was gone. Even if I knew sign language, my hands were totally useless. Once a day I managed to waggle my pinkie, not that anyone was paying attention. Why I was still on this earth I don't know. I was beyond helping any more of the departed. It sure was taking me a long time to die. These hospice gals had been coming for close to three months. I sure hoped I would regain my communication skills on the other side. In the meantime, looking back on my life was about all I had to pass what time I had left.

Fiction

A Good Egg

JUDITH FOURNIE HELMS

With the family gathered for the Fourth of July weekend, custom ordained each day's activities. The two younger sisters had planned their traditional July 5th morning stroll to the farmer's market. Both early risers, they were happy to tiptoe out of their parents' century-old colonial at 8 a. m. They strolled the familiar route to the town square at a leisurely pace, taking in countless reminders of growing up in the small Michigan town. As they entered the area of glorious displays of mounds and rows of reds, yellows, oranges, and greens, they stopped to admire the sheer bounty before them. Marnie paused to gather the courage to ask what she knew was a foolish question. "Listen, I just want to have realistic expectations, Lynne. So, is it basically a nagging toothache in your stomach, which peaks mid-week, then sort of dissipates until all the bleeding stops?"

"That's pretty close. It's so hard to capture pain in words." Lynne gently squeezed several tomatoes before placing two on the scale. "Listen, Marnie. It's nothing to worry about. Just discomfort and messiness for a week every month until you guys conceive. Tampons usually absorb what's shed. Then once you're pregnant, all of that goes away and you start the morning sickness."

"Great. So, from nagging stomach ache to active vomiting. Thanks, Sis. That makes me feel so much better."

"It's really not that horrible. And at the end, you have your baby." She winked.

Marnie studied her sister. Lynne looked exactly as she had eight months before, except for the large bulge between her breasts and her pubic bone, a lump accentuated by the pale pink knit shift she wore. As her sister handed the vendor a twenty, Marnie said, "I hope you're not sugar-coating it. Tom and I are dying to start trying, but, honestly, I'm not sure I can deal with all the pain."

Lynne wondered how her sister would endure childbirth if she was seriously worried about a few menstrual cycles. She took her change, thanked the vendor, and stuffed the small paper bag into the canvas tote slung over her shoulder. She laughed as they resumed their stroll. "Then it's lucky you didn't live in the olden days."

"What do you mean?"

"Just that twenty years ago women were still starting their periods at twelve or thirteen. And they didn't stop for, what? Thirty or forty years—until they went into menopause."

"Are you serious? Women were in pain a week out of every month for forty years?"

"Most were. Some in developed countries took pills that got it down to one week of menstruation every three months."

"Four periods a year. That's better than twelve."

"True. But most women didn't even get that relief."

"Let me guess. Just the privileged ones."

Her sister nodded. "And not that many of them, since people were always concerned about side-effects and long-term consequences. So, thank goodness for the shot." She glanced sideways at the twenty-two-year-old who was her mirror image—without the baby bump. "So, you really didn't know how it used to be?"

"Well, I knew cavewomen didn't have the shot. And it couldn't have been around in the 1960s or the Pill wouldn't have been such a big deal. But I did assume it had been around longer than twenty years."

"Hon, it wasn't widely available until 2030. Let's just say the playing field wasn't exactly level before that. Not to mention that abortions used to be a huge deal since birth control was seriously lacking. In fact, women used to be about evenly divided over whether abortions should even be legal. They called themselves 'pro-life' or 'pro-choice.'"

"Didn't it resolve when they realized women needed to band

together and demand that abortions shouldn't even be a thing?"

"Exactly. <u>Roe</u> wasn't going away, so the legal right to a first or second-term abortion was intact. But neither side had been persuaded that its moral argument was wrong."

"Wait. What's 'roe', again?"

"Darn it, Marnie. I told you that you should've taken a women's studies class, like the one I taught."

"Sorry." Marnie drew out the word.

Lynne shook her head, then smiled. "<u>Roe vs. Wade</u> was the U.S. Supreme Court case from 1973 that legalized abortion for the first two trimesters. After that decision came down, the pro-life folks dedicated themselves to overturning it since they thought all abortions were basically murder."

"How did women ever bridge that divide?"

"A lot of them eventually were able to see that the other side's argument could have merit, at the same time that their own position was correct. Male-dominated institutions didn't have the answers. It wasn't really the law that needed to change, anyway. It was science and medicine that had been ignoring women's obvious need for a solution. Women finally demanded one. And, in time, we got it."

"The shot."

"Yep."

"But 2030? Why did it take so long?"

"What do you think?"

"Organized resistance?"

"Of course."

"Men."

"No. Actually, it was mainly women."

"That's ridiculous. You're saying women clung to physical pain as well as the serious mental pain of unwanted pregnancies? Seriously?"

"Not exactly." Lynne noticed a tea and coffee booth with small metal tables around it, shaded by an awning. "Shall we get iced teas so we can talk this over before we head back to Mom's? I really don't want to discuss anything remotely touching on fertility within

Jessica's earshot."

"Sure. Mom told me last night they had another IVF failure. But I don't know the details." The women approached the counter, bought their iced drinks, and found an open table. After Marnie took a long sip, she said, "I really don't understand. Why would any woman have been against the shot?"

"It wasn't all women. A pretty small percentage, according to most sources. They had two worries. First, that if women were protected from pregnancy, girls would start having sex too early—and too often. And second, the official word from the Catholic Church, and a few other far-right ones, was that all contraception was immoral."

"Crazy. The same churches that were adamantly against abortion."

"Of course."

"It's actually amazing we ever got to where we are today."

"It is. At first, the scientific resources just weren't there—out of fear of backlash. But, over time, more and more people came to appreciate that women are just as entitled to use science and medicine to make their lives better as anyone else trying to improve on how nature dishes things out."

"Like fighting disease and repairing deformities. It's all just man fighting nature."

"Yeah. But a lot of people were hung up on the idea of women defying Mother Nature."

"I kind of understand that." She paused for a few moments and stared at her glass. "But the shot doesn't do anything but delay menstruation. So, it's not really a change—just a delay. How is it different from drugs that delay dementia, or slow down a cancer?"

"I know. And, eventually, most folks accepted it."

"And the concern that young women would become sluts?"

"False alarm. Of course."

Marnie rolled her eyes. "I could've told them it was."

"Most of us could have."

"Today, worrying about your daughter getting the shot is as anachronistic as worrying about her getting the polio vaccine. And the fact that it also eliminates menstruation until a woman wants to conceive is a huge bonus."

"I, for one, am thrilled to limit my dreaded periods to the months when Tom and I are trying to get pregnant. I just didn't realize it had been so controversial."

Lynne sighed and gently ran her fingers over her tummy. "Just the other day, I was thinking about all of this, and it hit me that it wouldn't have taken till 2030 to develop the shot if men had been getting periods and carrying unwanted embryos."

"Ha! You're probably right."

"Women ask for their rights. But men—well, they just take what they need."

"I'm just grateful to have it now."

"Yeah. I know."

Marnie was ready to change the subject. She pushed her glass back on the table and leaned in toward her sister. "Are you worried about Jessica?"

"It's a tough situation. She really had her hopes up since this was their fourth try at IVF. But she bombed again."

"How bad?"

"Only two eggs this time. And neither was a good prospect for fertilization."

"Crap. I hate to see her looking so unhappy. Especially when Tom and I are starting to try now—well, as soon as my periods start up. Maybe I won't tell her."

"Good idea. Not now, anyway."

"I'll wait as long as I can." She sighed. "I was just wondering. I get that her dearth of eggs is because of her age. But, like you were saying, there've been so many scientific advances. Surely there's something else Jessica can try?"

"Yeah. I wish she'd just use one of Grandma's frozen embryos like Mom...." Lynne abruptly turned away. She said under her breath, "Never mind."

"Wait. What? Mom conceived using her parents' frozen embryo?"

"No. Of course not."

"Lynne?"

"Possibly. I mean, I'm not sure."

"Lynne?"

"You'd really have to ask her."

"Lynne. Stop acting like that!"

"Like what?"

"Like you're afraid to divulge the nuclear code. All I want to know is what you meant when you said Mom used her mom's frozen embryo to conceive."

Lynne bit her bottom lip and stared into space for what seemed an eternity to Marnie. Eventually, she sighed and said, "I guess it's out of the bag now."

"Kind of."

"You mustn't tell anyone what I'm about to tell you."

"No deal. I have to tell Tom."

Lynne stared at her. "Okay. But no one else."

"Fine."

"You have to promise."

"What do you want? A pinkie-swear? Fine." She stuck out her little finger.

Lynne ignored it. "It's just that Mom swore me to secrecy. I personally think you have a right to know. But, it's Mom's secret to share with whomever she chooses. I didn't mean to let her down. Honestly, it just slipped out."

"Listen, Lynne. That falls into the category of your problem. My problem is that I'm having a crisis here—wondering about my very identity. So, I'm sorry I can't commiserate with you about your slip-up. But if you don't tell me right now what's going on, I may have a melt-down."

"What do you mean by that?"

"Screaming. Jumping on the table. Throwing things."

"Oh, don't be so dramatic."

"Tell me."

"All right. After Jessica and I were born, Mom and Dad tried for another baby. Jessica and I got the feeling they were hoping for a boy, but I don't remember why we had that sense." Marnie sat quietly, eyes riveted to her sister. "Anyway, years went by. Finally, they tried IVF—I think it was three tries."

"They were sharing this with you?"

"Oh, yeah. Mom was always very open about things like sex and fertility. When the last IVF failed, they started working with a new fertility specialist. He wanted them to use a donor egg and Dad's sperm."

"That's not unusual. Right?"

"Right. But Mom wouldn't have it. She believed the baby should have 23 chromosomes from each of them, or they should move on to try to adopt."

"Am I adopted?"

"No." She shook her head. "It had been almost three years, and all three of the birth-mothers they worked with had changed their minds about giving up their babies after the births. Mom was getting really depressed over it. Jessica and I could see it was eating at her, but there was nothing we could do."

"Hm."

"So, one evening, Grandma called the house and asked for Mom and Dad to stop by to see them the next day. We girls weren't invited, and we weren't told what it was about."

"Mysterious."

"Yeah. So, about three months later, Mom was pregnant with you."

"Did she and Dad seem disappointed I wasn't a boy?"

"Not in the least."

"Good. I'd hate to have been a disappointment at such a young age. So, somehow you figured out that Grandma had donated a frozen embryo to them?"

"Of course not. When I was around sixteen, and you were six, I was snooping around the attic looking for my old scrapbooks, and I found the paperwork about it."

"Did you tell Mom you knew?"

"I did. I mean, I didn't plan to. But I couldn't live with it without talking with someone."

"What did she say?"

"That was the funny thing. She didn't say much. She acted like it was no big deal. She said something like, 'Families come together in all different ways. Lots of couples use IVF, others surrogacy, and some turn to adoption. Your father and I decided to see if I could carry an embryo that had been cryopreserved.'"

"How did you respond to that?"

"Oh, the usual. Something like, 'What the hell are you talking about? Is Marnie my grandparents' child? Wouldn't that make her your sister, Mom?'"

"Jesus."

"She remained very calm. She said, 'Don't be silly, Lynne. Marnie is as much my daughter as you are.' So I said, 'I meant genetically. She's your sister, Mom!'"

"Oh, my."

"Mom went on to explain how she and Dad look at it. She said, 'Do you think you'd be any less our child if you were adopted, Lynne?' So I said, 'No,' because I was pretty sure they would've felt exactly the same about me if they'd adopted me. Then she said, 'Marnie is every bit as much our baby as if I'd delivered her after she'd been conceived with my own egg and your father's sperm. I've had a baby in my arms both ways, and I can assure you, there's no difference.'"

"But, Lynne, if it was so inconsequential in her mind, why was it kept a secret?"

"Good question. She said it was because there are ignorant people in the world who might try to hurt you with it."

"That's it?"

"That's it."

"Wow." Marnie took a long, deep breath. "But I look so much like you and Jessica."

"True. I guess we all take after Mom's side of the family." She laughed.

"I'd say so." She paused to let it all soak in. "But one thing doesn't make sense."

"One thing?"

"Ha. Here's what I'm wondering. If Mom didn't want to carry

an embryo that had 23 chromosomes from another woman, how did she come to accept this one—me—that had none of her or Dad's input?"

Lynne lightly patted her tummy with her fingertips as she thought. "Remember, she didn't want Dad's sperm to fertilize another woman's egg. But this embryo...." She smiled. "I mean you. Well, you weren't conceived using the genetic material of either of them, since it was all from Mom's parents."

"Then all of my genes were from Mom's side of the family."

"True. But Dad wasn't really objecting to anything. I think if Mom had had a good egg, and needed sperm other than Dad's to fertilize it, he'd have been fine with that. I gathered that he just wanted to have a third child."

"Thank goodness they didn't go that route."

"Why?"

"Duh! Because I'd never have come into existence."

"Good point. But you wouldn't have known, because you wouldn't exist."

"That makes me feel better, Lynne." Marnie smiled. "Here's an idea. What if Mom hadn't had embryo-me implanted, and I'd just hung out in the freezer?"

"Then you'd still have a chance at being chosen by someone for implantation."

"Someone like Jessica?"

"Shit. That's true."

"Wait. So then, genetically, I'd be grandmother's daughter, Mom's sister, your aunt, and Jessica's aunt, except that Jessica would also be like my surrogate mother."

"Maybe."

"Now, let's assume that I'm me, Mom's daughter, and, genetically, her sister."

"Right."

"So, if Jessica were to make use of another of our grandparents' frozen embryos, to develop into her child, let's say it's a girl...."

"Good chance."

"Well, Lynne, wouldn't the child be Jessica's daughter and, genetically, our mom's sister—like me? So, I'd be the little girl's aunt, but genetically her sister. Right?" Marnie smiled broadly.

Lynne burst out laughing and sputtered, "I'm sorry. That just struck me as funny. But I know it's not, Marnie."

Marnie acted wounded for a moment, and then said, "Are you kidding?" She burst out laughing and Lynne joined in.

When they finally stopped, Lynne said, "But I really want to know. How do you honestly feel about all of this?"

Marnie looked out across the crowds now filling the market area—adults in shorts and flip-flops, children trying to contain their exuberant dogs on bright-colored leashes, and babies in strollers and back-carriers. "I agree with Mom. The baby is the whole story. Couples don't agonize about whose egg and sperm came together to emerge as the child they adopted. So, it's really just a curiosity to me that Grandma's egg and Grandpa's sperm started me out. Our parents' third child just as easily could have been the genetic product of stranger A and stranger B, if one of their adoption attempts had worked out."

Lynne reached out and held her sister's hands over the small table. "So, you're really okay?"

"Actually, I'm thrilled—and extremely grateful to Grandma that she held on to my cryopreserved little embryo body." She shook her head. "But, I am glad I didn't know before."

"Why?"

"When I was little, I was jealous of you and Jessica for being so close. I probably would've lorded it over you that I was the only kid who was also Mom's sister."

"Yeah. You probably would've."

"It's actually a pretty cool story. Maybe, after Tom and I have our baby, I'll tease Mom with 'sister' birthday cards."

"Honestly, I think she'd love that." She paused. "But don't tell Jessica."

"Hey. I think I pinkie-swore not to."

"It's just that it's still Mom's secret to share."

"Right. But I hope Mom shares it soon. It's about time Jessica has my sister."

Fiction

MARIE'S MARIE

JUDITH FOURNIE HELMS

"The beach vacations always frighten me a little. I warn my grandchildren about those…" She paused. "…Forces in the ocean that pull you out to sea," said Marie.

"Rip-tides," said Eve.

"Right. Rip-tides," replied Marie, starting the laughter that followed the women's word-retrieval failures.

Their thirty-something waitress approached the table. "You two always have the best time—and you don't even drink much wine. What's the deal?"

Eve said, "We could tell you, but then we'd have to kill you." Marie nodded solemnly.

"Got it. Your secret." She smiled at the older women. "Would you like coffee or dessert?"

Marie ordered their usual, then turned back to her friend. "Listen, Eve, I have something to confess."

"Oh, I hope it's a love affair."

"I wish it were. I still miss David every darn day. But I'm not opposed to finding someone. Mr. Right just doesn't seem to be on the prowl for a sixty-five-year-old retiree.

"In that case, I hope you've planned a fabulous cruise vacation. A good way to meet Cary Grant, if I'm remembering correctly," replied Eve.

"No. I would've invited you."

"Of course, you would've," said Eve as she patted her friend's hand. Retirement suited Eve very well. With freckles and perpetually red hair, she appeared to be a decade younger than her sixty-seven years. "We would share Cary Grant, of course, if we stumbled across him." Eve licked her lips.

"Don't be vulgar," said Marie. With Eve just staring at her, she added, "Okay. Fine. Be vulgar."

"So tell me. What's your confession?"

"Okay. Here's the thing. Even though I really was quite adept with words as a trial lawyer, they seem to be deserting me now, day by day."

"That's it?" said Eve. "All our friends have word-retrieval issues. I don't think it's anything to worry about."

"Listen, what I'm telling you is just the backdrop. But, it's a backdrop you need to know. My memory is really getting worse. When we're together, I've just been censoring myself not to talk about anything that includes a word I can't easily access." When Eve raised her eyebrows,

Marie added, "Rip-tides just slipped through."

"You're serious."

"As serious as a progressive disease."

"Is that what you think it is?"

"Probably. Dementia or Alzheimers."

"Shouldn't you see a doctor?"

"I already have. She said the loss may be sporadic, so I may have weeks or months when it slows down. I'm supposed to check in with her again in six months."

"I'm so sorry," said Eve. "Is there anything I can do?"

"Not about the memory thing." Marie paused and looked down at the table for a few moments. "But there is something I'd like you to help me with." When she looked up, Eve couldn't help but notice how her brown page-boy with short bangs accentuated her hazel eyes and shapely brows. It was a youthful style that still looked good on her. Marie folded her hands on the table and leaned in.

"So, what's going on, Marie?"

Marie took a long breath. "I want to find my birth-mother."

Eve shook her head. "You mean a birth-child, right?"

"No. I've managed to keep *mother* and *child* differentiated—so far." She smiled. "I'd like to find my biological mother while I still know who I am."

"Wow. How come you never told me you were adopted?"

"It wasn't a big secret, Eve. My grammar school friends, who were also my high school friends, all knew. But when I moved to Chicago for college and law school, it never seemed important enough to bring up with the people I met."

"But, did you think much about it as a child? I mean, didn't you wonder why she didn't keep you?"

The waitress returned and managed to serve the coffees and the dessert without interrupting the women. Marie smiled at her and then returned her attention to Eve. "My parents were great about that. They explained that she couldn't take care of me, so she made a plan for me. She thought they would be wonderful parents for me. And they really were. I was always a busy bee, so I didn't have time to think more about it. Who knows? Maybe I was such a crazy overachiever so I wouldn't have to. It wasn't until much later that I started to get curious."

"How much later?"

"It was when I had my babies."

"Tony and Tina are around thirty-five, right?"

"Thirty-six this September."

"They were just sweet sixteen last year!" said Eve. "So, what were you feeling then?"

"It hit me that my adoptive parents were my real parents—the ones who paced the floor soothing me at night, changed my poopy diapers, and guided me through absolutely everything in my life. Once I was a mother, I understood what it really means to be one. And I knew my biological mother was never one—at least, not to me."

"I can see that," said Eve. "So why now?"

"This will sound do-gooderish. But the truth is, I want to find her for her, not for me. I'd just like to give her the gift of knowing I had a good life—to ease her conscience, in case it's been bothering her. And, if I'm going to do it, it has to be now."

"Have you started looking?"

"Yeah. I entered my info in some of the registries—but no luck. As you know, my folks are both gone. Since I didn't have any siblings, no one else has any family memorabilia. All I have to go on is my birth certificate from St. Margaret's Hospital with my adoptive parents' names on it, the date and time of my birth, and my length and weight."

"Wait. It should have the name of the doctor who delivered you."

"You're right, Eve. It does. Dr. Michael Husman."

"He's dead. Right?"

"Yes. Twenty-five years ago! I just don't know where to go from here."

"I have some ideas."

"Great!" Marie smiled at her. "What do I do?"

"First, publish a letter in the local newspapers. Include all of the information you have. A terrible long-shot, but it can't hurt."

"I like it, Eve. I'll start working on it tomorrow. What else do you have?"

"You need to go down there."

"To Belleville?"

"Yes. You need to show up at the office of the director of the hospital's records department to tell your story. Let's just hope you find a sympathetic ear."

Marie said, "Want to travel to southern Illinois with me?"

"Of course. And since I worked labor and delivery for over three decades, I know the usual procedures and the lingo." She smiled. "I'm in."

"Oh, thanks so much." Marie leaned over and gave her a hug. "I should've done this sooner. But until I retired, I barely made time to sleep. And after I lost David, I didn't have the willpower for a couple of years. Now that I'm ready, my mind has decided I need to put this assignment on a rocket-docket." She sighed. "I don't know if we'll get anywhere. I just want to give it a try."

***

Marie remembered the hospital's horseshoe-shaped entrance driveway from when she'd last been in town, thirty-five years earlier. The women's heels clicked as they crossed the marble floor in the lobby to the reception desk. Eve asked for the director of medical records and was told that, without an appointment, it could be a while. After forty minutes, a fifty-something woman in a navy pantsuit walked up to them. "Hello, I'm Sally Stutzman. Let's go down to my office." They followed her down a gleaming, freshly-waxed, tile hallway and into her office. It had a window to a forested back area of the grounds.

"Lovely view," said Marie.

Sally smiled. "Yes. And I really must make time to glance at it once in a while." She sat behind her small mahogany desk and motioned to the two upholstered visitor chairs. "Please, make yourselves comfortable. What can I do for you ladies?"

Marie introduced herself and mentioned that Eve was a retired nurse. She told her story—without including her fading memory. Ms. Stutzman listened patiently, then smiled kindly before she spoke. "I'm sorry, Marie. But even if I could find a birth record from 1952, there's no way I could share it with anyone except the patient, herself." Marie sighed audibly. Ms. Stutzman continued, "I admire what you're doing, Marie. If I could find the records, and if the law allowed me to give them to you, I'd be very happy to."

Hoping she wouldn't alienate the director, Marie tried a different strategy. "As a lawyer, I do know there are ways to get around laws."

"Not in this case."

"How can you be so sure?" asked Eve.

"There was a flood in the basement back in the sixties. All of our birth records were lost. I'm sorry, but you've wasted your trip. Is there anything else I can do?"

Eve stood and said, "May I speak with you privately for a moment?"

Ms. Stutzman glanced at Marie, and then said, "Of course."

Marie rose. "You mustn't give up your office. I'll let myself out. Thanks so much for your time, Ms. Stutzman."

Ten minutes later, when Eve got back to the lobby, Marie asked, "What was that all about?"

"Just nurse-to-nurse talk."

"Did you get anything?"

"No. But she took my cell number in case she thinks of anything that might help."

"Legally?"

"Of course."

The two women walked over to the address that had belonged to Dr. Husman. They explained to the elderly office manager that they wanted to see birth records from 1952. The woman laughed out loud, then quickly apologized. She explained that Dr. Husman's records had been preserved for five years after his death in 1993, so patients would have sufficient time to request copies before the records were destroyed. She went on to explain that the record retention approach they settled on had been approved by a court.

Eve responded, "We're not complaining about anything. We were just hoping the records might still exist."

"I am sorry," said the office manager.

Since it was still too early for lunch, Eve and Marie walked down Main Street to the offices of the local newspaper. Marie decided to post her open letter as an advertisement, rather than put it in the classified section. It cost more, but she imagined it would have a better chance of being seen. The ad was to run for two weeks, weekdays and Sundays. Marie reviewed what she'd typed up with the clerk and paid the price for the period of publication.

As they left the newspaper office, Marie said, "So, we've completed all of our tasks, and it isn't even noon on Day 1. Do you want to spend the night or head back to Chicago?"

"Oh, let's spend the night. After lunch, show me all your old haunts."

"I can show you some," said Marie. "Others, like my bucolic high school campus, have been demolished in favor of a strip mall."

"Then show me where it was." Eve smiled.

The women shared a room at a new Holiday Inn Express. After a long day of sight-seeing in Belleville, they'd decided to turn in early and then drive back to Chicago the following day. It was after

11 p.m., and both women were asleep when Eve's phone buzzed. She reached for it on the night stand and finally was able to get her fingers around it in the dark. "Hello."

"Hello, Eve? This is Sally Stutzman."

"Wait. Are you still at work, Sally?"

"Actually, I am."

"You poor thing. Why are you working so late?"

"For your friend."

Eve sat up. "Really? Do you have something for us?"

"Listen. As I told you, the records are long gone. But I had another thought. There was a nurse who was here forever—in labor and delivery for most of her tenure. Her name was Milicent Rogers. She retired at seventy—almost twenty years ago. I chatted with her many times over the decades we overlapped here. Very religious—I recall that she always wore a little gold cross on a chain. As far as I know, she never married."

"Do you know where she is now?"

"That's why I'm still sitting in my office. I got the information I needed from old personnel files. Then I did some sleuthing. She's at Our Lady of Perpetual Light."

"What's that?"

"A Catholic retirement village. It's just outside of town—I can text you the directions."

"You think Milicent may remember something about Marie?"

"I don't know. My guess is, only if the circumstances were unusual. It's impossible to remember it all."

"Of course. May I ask you something, Sally?"

"Sure."

"Why are you helping us?"

"We're fellow nurses. And when you told me about Marie's deterioration, it brought back memories of my own mother. I've been thinking that if she'd been on one last quest, I sure hope someone would've helped her."

"She's gone?"

"Yes."

"I'm so sorry."

"Me too. And by the way, if you tell anyone I gave you this information, I'll deny I've ever met you."

"You're a stranger to me."

"Perfect."

"Thanks, Sally."

"You're very welcome."

In the morning, Marie and Eve had an early breakfast at the hotel buffet and then, following Sally's directions, headed for the retirement home. As they made their way down the long, main driveway, they saw rolling hills, lush gardens, grottoes, and a winding path featuring the Stations of the Cross. The home was a large, red-brick, colonial-style building. Upon entering, they approached the receptionist and introduced themselves. She said her name was Janice and asked how she could help. They asked if they might visit with Milicent Rogers.

"Are you relatives?"

"No," said Eve.

"Friends?"

"I hope we will be," said Marie.

"I'm terribly sorry, ladies. But I must ask the nature of your interest in Milicent. We don't allow solicitors, and it's my job to protect the privacy of our residents."

"We're not solicitors," said Eve.

"The truth is, I'm trying to locate my birth-mother," said Marie.

"And you think Milicent…."

"No," said Eve. Both she and Marie shook their heads. Eve continued, "We've been told that Milicent was a labor and delivery nurse at the Catholic hospital in town—for many years. We're hoping she may remember something about Marie's birth."

"She may be willing to talk with you. Milicent is perfectly competent to decide for herself. I'll just explain what you've told me and leave it up to her."

"Wonderful," said Marie.

"Like many of our residents, she has difficulty recalling recent events. But she often tells detailed stories of things that happened long ago. Please have a seat, and I'll stop by her apartment. I just have to get someone to cover for me here first."

Fifteen minutes had passed when Eve and Marie saw Janice approach, pushing someone in a wheelchair. The resident had very thin, very white hair and a pink complexion, and she looked quite frail in spite of the bright smile on her face. A delicate gold chain with a tiny cross was settled between her prominent collar bones, just above the lace collar of her blouse. Both women rose from their chairs as the wheelchair was pushed to a spot directly opposite them. "Hello, I'm Milicent. Who are you?"

Eve took her hand and spoke softly. "I'm Eve, and this is my friend, Marie."

"Well, thank you for coming to see me. I understand you have a question for me about when I was working at St. Margaret's."

As they sat back down, Marie explained what she knew from her birth certificate. Milicent sat quietly and listened. Once Marie had finished, the elderly woman said, "Let me just think for a moment."

"Of course," said Eve.

Milicent wrinkled her brow and squeezed her eyes closed. She sighed a couple of times as the wall clock ticked off the minutes. After a while, Milicent looked at Marie. "I am so sorry to disappoint you. But you are asking me about 1952. Why, that was sixty-five years ago! If there were just something unusual about it, I might recall it. But for a young woman to give a baby up for adoption was actually quite common back then. That was before the pill and before the dreadful abortions became so popular. So, there were a fair number of placements. I'm sorry."

Eve and Marie glanced at each other. Marie rose and said, "Thank you so much for meeting with us. It was very kind of you." She looked up at the receptionist who was still standing behind the wheelchair. "And thank you as well...."

"Marie?" said Milicent.

"Yes?"

"Is that you?"

Marie looked from the receptionist to Eve for a clue, and then back to Milicent. "I'm Marie Mattigan. We just met a few minutes ago."

The elderly woman gaped around as though she'd become confused. Looking at Marie, she said, "You're the one who had to give up your baby, aren't you?"

"No," said Marie patiently. "I'm trying to find the woman who gave me up."

The elderly woman laughed. "How silly of me. Marie would be almost eighty. You must be her daughter."

All three women surrounding her got goose bumps. Milicent continued, "It's your nose, dear. Marie had an unusual ski-jump nose—like Bob Hope, only feminine. She was very pretty. When I saw you look up at Janice, I caught a good look at you. You must understand how I mistook you for Marie."

Eve and Marie pulled their chairs up closer to Milicent. Janice knelt on the floor at her knee to hear her story. "Tell us," said Janice. "Tell us what you remember."

She leaned toward the younger women. "She was a local girl. Went to St. Timothy's where she was just in eighth grade. One day, she took a short-cut home from a friend's house, up over the railroad tracks. She was attacked. The man—a vagabond—had his way with her and left her on the side of the tracks. Once she made her way home, she was so ashamed that she didn't tell anyone. She finally told her story when she started showing. By then, the man was long gone. A good thing, probably. She had a brother who kept guns for hunting. She thought he might've killed the man if he'd ever found him. Marie wanted to become a nun."

"Because of the rape?" asked Eve.

"No. She'd always planned to go into the convent after eighth grade."

"So, this story was common knowledge back then?" asked Marie.

"Oh my, no. I learned all of it while I was tending Marie for the childbirth. When I saw her, so young and so beautiful the one time she held her baby, it struck me that she looked like Mary holding Our Lord. I guess that's why I remembered her story. That image stayed with me. And when I saw your profile—why, you're her spittin' image."

"Where did she go for high school?' asked Eve.

"St. Louis. One of the novitiates in St. Louis is what she mentioned to me."

"Do you remember what order she planned to join?"

"No." Milicent sat and thought for a couple of minutes. "No. I'm sorry. If she mentioned it, I don't remember."

"Can you tell me her last name?" said Marie.

"No. I'm sorry. No idea."

"Well, what you've shared was a huge help, Milicent. Is there anything else?" said Eve.

"She was a godly girl. She told me that once she told her family what had happened, she was able to accept it as God's will. I imagine she did become a nun. She would've been a good one."

Driving back to their hotel, Eve and Marie knew they were too emotionally spent to undertake the trip back to Chicago. So, they stayed one more night at the hotel.

"I wish I'd brought my laptop," said Eve.

"Me, too. I can't wait to get home and begin my search for the convents. If we get close, will you come back with me—to St. Louis?"

"Try to stop me!"

Marie pulled her covers up and fell into a deep, dreamless sleep. Eve crept over to the little desk and made outlines and diagrams of the steps she'd take to find Marie's Marie.

***

A week later, the women were sitting in Eve's study, working on their laptops to find the woman Milicent had described. "I've got it!" said Eve.

"What?"

"This may be it. Missionary Servants of St. John. They trained novices in St. Louis in the 1950s and 1960s. Some of the girls were put through college, always at DePaul or Loyola in Chicago.

It looks like their nuns were placed all over the globe, mainly at orphanages."

"Are they still operating?"

"It says their motherhouse is outside Madison, Wisconsin."

"But, Eve, why do you think this is the one?"

"Because we've checked out the other five possibilities and gotten nowhere."

"Not a very good reason."

"It's all I've got. Shall I call Madison?"

"No. I'll do it."

"Okay. Here's the number. Good luck."

Marie took a deep breath and dialed. "Hello, this is Marie Mattigan. May I speak with the Mother Superior?"

"One moment please."

When the Mother Superior answered, Marie explained how she had gotten to where she was in her search and was told that the convent had files on all of their 112 sisters. The Mother Superior said she'd be happy to look through them to see if anything seemed to match up. A couple of hours later, she called Marie back. "I may have something."

"So soon?"

"Well, I decided to start with the sisters who have Marie as a part of the name they chose when they took their orders. Of course, that only narrowed it to 50 since Marie is very popular with the sisters. After that, I focused on dates of birth. From your story, the sister would have to have been born in the late 1930s. That got me down to four sisters, three of whom have already gone to their heavenly reward."

"Is there any reason to believe that the fourth could be my birth-mother?"

"Not really. Sister Marie Rose did have an interesting life: trained with us in St. Louis, finished college in Chicago, and majored in Spanish and French. We wanted our young women to be prepared for their assignments. Then she worked at our orphanage in Haiti for almost 56 years. She became our director there in 1970 and stayed until she fell and suffered a hip fracture in 2016." She paused. "I just wish you'd found us a year or two ago. Sister has been losing her memory since her hospitalization, and the loss has accelerated in the past year. I'm afraid she's been diagnosed with Alzheimers."

Marie said, "Do you think she could be the one?"

"I really don't know. The dates fit, as does the connection with St. Louis. But all of that could be coincidences. Why don't you come by and visit with her?"

"Really? May I?"

"Oh, yes. Sister loves visitors and has precious few. So, at the very least, you'll be doing a kindness for her."

"Thank you so much. Would tomorrow be too soon?"

"Tomorrow would be lovely. But remember, she fades in and out of lucidity, so you may not even catch her in a moment of clarity to ask your questions. She may very well be in a place where we can't reach her."

"I understand. My friend Eve and I will be there tomorrow."

Marie had a big smile on her face as she turned to Eve. "Tomorrow." Then Marie explained what she'd learned about Sister Marie Rose's history and her illness. "I hope it's she, Eve."

"Me, too. But please don't get your hopes up. It's rather a long shot. Honestly, I can't believe the head nun was so helpful."

"I guess I just thought she acted like a person married to God should act."

"Good point. What time shall I pick you up?"

***

As the two women stepped into the old brick building, they were both struck by the silence. Their footsteps were the only sound as they approached the reception desk. They were taken to meet the Mother Superior in her office. After brief introductions, the three of them walked down a long hallway to Sister Marie Rose's room. She was sitting up in a recliner. It was situated just to the side of her single bed, over which hung a crucifix. The only other furniture was a small, oak chest of drawers near the door.

She was small and looked as frail as a sickly sparrow. As she wore the traditional garb, only her weathered face could be seen. Marie studied the nun's nose, hoping to see a reflection of her own, but just couldn't be sure. One of the sisters came in to set up folding chairs, and the three women sat down to talk with Sister Marie Rose.

"Good morning, Sister," said the Mother Superior. "I've brought you two visitors." Sister Marie Rose looked up, but her eyes failed to focus on the women. "Go ahead and tell her your story, Marie."

Marie cleared her throat. Her heart was racing, but she was able to lay out all of the facts she'd gathered. There was no response. Eve tried. She reminded Sister Marie Rose of the interesting and altruistic life the woman had lived, and of how much good she surely did in Haiti. Although Eve was speaking, the sister was facing in Marie's direction. However, her stare seemed to be focused inward. Eve received no response.

Mother Superior turned the conversation to the weather and then the choral work the sisters were doing to prepare for celebratory masses. Sister Marie Rose simply sat and ignored the world outside herself. After thirty minutes, Mother Superior said, "Sister, you should rest now. Perhaps Marie and Eve will visit you again."

Marie said, "Oh, we would love to." She reached out to take the elderly nun's hand to say goodbye, knowing that she'd blown it. She'd waited too long.

"I know who you are," said Sister Marie Rose. The nun's eyes seemed to be focusing on Marie.

Marie's mouth dropped, and she leaned over to hug the woman. When Marie released the nun from the embrace, there were tears in Marie's eyes, but no sign of recognition in Sister Marie Rose's. The women sat with her for another half hour, hoping for another moment of clarity. There was nothing left for them.

As they drove back to Chicago, Eve and Marie spoke of nothing but the sister's utterance. Marie dared to hope it was meaningful but knew well it might have been random. She and Eve tried to convince themselves there would be more connection on future visits.

Marie had arranged to stop by the convent for another visit in a few days and was anxious for the time to pass quickly so she could try again. Two days later, she received a call from the Mother Superior, letting her know that Sister Marie Rose had passed away. Marie doubled over, sobbing. Once she regained her composure, she picked up the phone she'd dropped on the floor. "I'm so sorry. I'm crying as though the sister actually was my birth-mother. But I don't even know. I'm sorry for your loss, Mother."

"Marie," said the Mother Superior. "There's something you should know."

"Please tell me. I don't think I can take any more suspense."

"Well, dear, I'm afraid you'll have to. This isn't something I can tell you. It's something I need to show you."

Marie took a deep breath. "I'm on my way." Marie called Eve right away, but there was no answer. Unable to bear delay, she went alone.

The Mother Superior was in the lobby when Marie arrived two hours later. She led Marie into her office and asked her to take a seat on the small couch. "When Sister Marie Rose came to us for her retirement, she brought with her a small, locked leather satchel. She wore the key to it around her neck. She asked me to keep it for her and not to bother about it until her death. I opened it this morning, and I'd like to give it to you."

"To me?"

The Mother Superior picked up the satchel from her desk and presented it to her. Marie's mouth was dry, and her hands trembled as she accepted it. The satchel was as weathered as Sister Marie Rose's face had been, with hundreds of tiny lines coursing its surface. Small bits of the leather leafed off when she lifted the flap.

Marie pulled out the contents and set them on her lap. She saw herself staring back. There were familiar pictures of her as a baby, a toddler holding a teddy bear, in her First Communion dress, and all of her grade school pictures. High school, college and law school graduation photos condensed her life, but the powerful memories they evoked reinflated it. There was also an 8" by 10" of a favorite wedding picture and a simple faded snapshot of her in 1982, in full bloom carrying the twins. That was the last photo in the pile. When Marie turned them over, she was shocked to see her adoptive mother's handwriting. She had written on the back of each photo, "Our Marie," followed by a date. That last photo was dated May 1982, a month before her adoptive mother had died. Stunned and wordless, Marie just stared at the pile of photographs. It was several minutes before she looked up. She said, "I found her, didn't I?"

"Yes, Marie. You found her."

"She saw me, didn't she?"

"I believe she did. When Sister Marie Rose said, 'I know who you are,' she'd made her way out of the fog."

"I suppose I really hadn't needed to find her after all. She'd always known I had a good life."

"Yes. But I do think she held onto hers until she'd gotten to meet you."

Poetry

Algorithm

LAWRENCE HELMS

He glanced at the clock—it said three pm,
About good a time as any
To bring the whole thing to an end,
Since it had played out plenty.

He thought it odd that when it came,
It carried so scant emotion.
He had no one to thank or blame;
He'd avoided such commotion.

So as he started preparations,
He idly thought it through—
Why life with so few perturbations
Led to what he'd do.

But he was never one to dwell,
And soon he redirected,
Patting the dog to say farewell.
Then, as their eyes connected,

He thought he saw it as it was—
Present now in living,
Eyes with more than dumb-dog trust—
Possibly forgiving.

The man then came to pivot place,
Stirred by dog's black eyes—
Will he be saved by dogged grace,
Or will the man still die?

Fiction

Quick Bite

LAWRENCE HELMS

"So I said to him, 'Who the hell isn't a spokesman?' He was giving me that crap about how a person makes choices and we owe it to ourselves and to the whole of humankind to make good choices and blah blah blah. Said I know what I'm doing's wrong, that I don't believe a word of it, that I'm lending my talents to greed and evil blah blah. 'Course, I came right back at him with my sure-fire shot—'You're a lawyer and you're laying this crap on me? At least I have a point of view to present, and I stick with it and present it well. You'll take any point of view for $250 an hour, any point of view, mind you, even if you took the opposite one that morning, maybe for $225 because that's a more regular customer. So where do you get off looking down at me?'

"And he gave me the same tired tripe about how his role is to put out there his client's best case, and there's a lawyer on the other side putting out his client's best case, and there's a neutral arbiter weighing it all and coming up with a decision based on fair consideration of both sides. Said mine is different because I'm talking to a gullible public, not a trained judge. And that I have an unfair advantage from the huge resources of my evil master (well, he calls it my company, but I know damn well he's thinking evil master). Said there's no comparison. No comparison! What a crock. So I said it's exactly the same and a blind fool can see that. I lay out the best case in favor of my industry, lay it out to the consuming public. All the hand-wringers and tree-huggers and Kumbaya types have their own spokespeople getting their little weaselly message out there to the same public. The public chooses. So I nailed him, 'You saying the American public is dumber than those hacks in the Daley Center? How many times have you groused to me about how stupid it is to elect judges? How many times have you told me the ones that run are the lawyers who couldn't make it as lawyers?' And he hemmed and hawed and did that little phlegm sound he does and said he never said all of them are bad. So I stuck it to him and said, 'Not all the public's stupid and gullible, either. They can decide whether to be influenced by our position or not.'"

She has been sitting, nodding occasionally, picking up the greens from her plate. She is thinking of the parent-teacher meeting set for five, worrying over what she fears will be another not-so-good report while worrying, just a little less, about having to leave at 3:30 to get to the North Shore on time. She can tell enough by his inflection to pick up if he asks her a question or invites a comment. She pays no more attention than is necessary to pull this off. In fact, she knows she lets her attention flag below this level at times, because she trusts from experience that he is unlikely to ask her anything or invite her comment. She calls these his "soliloquies." They almost always involve some instance of a challenge to him, or what he perceives as a challenge, almost always from another male. She shifts focus from the parent-teacher conference to wondering if he'd be having the very same conversation in his head if he hadn't asked her to meet him for a quick bite. It was the last thing she wanted; she needed to stay at her desk, especially since she has to leave early, with the report due tomorrow. But he'd had that plaintive edge in his voice, like he needed her. Needed to try, somehow. She'd thought it might even have something to do with Jason and the conference. That was why she came out to meet him, in fact; must have been. Some half-coalesced sense he was concerned about the conference. Concerned about Jason. She thinks how silly she was, that of course it was just agitation over another perceived slight, and that he needed—not her, just an audience.

He is still talking. Same soliloquy, same cadence, same indignation. She lets her thought emerge more. She had <u>hoped</u> it was about Jason. She had hoped he felt bad about his umpteenth feeble excuse as to why he couldn't make it with her to the conference. New initiative on "assisting" public perception of the pipeline or something. Hugely important. The public awaits the next million-dollar whitewash barrage with eager anticipation, hunger even. For the half-truths and zero-truths. Yeah.

She realizes that she's down to the last grape tomato on her plate, cuts it, and eats one half, then the other. She sees he's only about half through the thick sandwich, his usual determined and down-gazing consumption having been slowed by his monologue. Not slowed enough, though, to make his eating method more palatable, she thinks. There's a bit of mayonnaise in the corner of his mouth. He's been speaking right through his chewing of the large bites of sandwich.

She thinks her finishing of her meal gives her a valid reason to deliver herself from his stream of wounded consciousness. He'd said they'd just get a quick bite. It amazes and angers her that she even considers whether it will be rude to leave. She's struck by the thought that she can't recall allowing the anger part for some time. Why does she allow herself to be put upon and then work to make sure she's gracious about being put upon?

She looks at him. The mayonnaise is gone, for which she is grateful. But the lips are still moving, the jaw is chewing. The stiff, pristine white collar is like a pipe from which his neck overflows and muffin-tops; she recalls when his neck emerged strong and straight from the collar.

She senses the change in inflection and scrambles to retrieve the words she hopes have lodged somewhere in her consciousness. He's asked a question. Wonder of wonders. She's momentarily close to flustering, but she regains herself as the echo reveals itself. He has asked, "Am I right?"

She has heard the question before. Many times. This time, though, it really annoys her. Not like it has for at least five years now. It really annoys her. No, it angers her. All this in the moment they look at each other. She sees the look, the impatient one, on his face. "Haven't you been listening to me?" he asks.

It is so unlike what she has felt before. No, unlike what she has allowed herself to feel. It moves with a quiver through her chest and radiates up and down through her arms and legs, toes, and fingers. It is visceral, electric, current under resistance, hitting her head inside and out, raising her brows and tensing her upper lip.

"No, Carlton, I have not been listening. I haven't been listening for several years now. I doubt I'll be listening again, either."

She sees his eyelids rise, thinks she sees his pupils pulse and dilate, though she continues talking.

"But I heard your question. No, you're not right. You are so not right. You're…"

She sees his amazement transform to anger in a flash. She realizes, with the new shudder through her which she senses is a sort of joy, that she does not feel distressed by the anger. She sees him put down the remaining part of the sandwich and thinks, "Got his attention."

She hears him hiss, "For God's sake, Justine, keep your voice down. People are…"

"No, Carl. It's been down long enough. I'm surprised it even still has a higher volume. But it does, thank God." Her voice goes loud enough that everyone looks their way, although only he seems to notice.

"I was saying, Carl, you're not right. You've been wrong so long now. And, and… Right now you're thinking (if you can think while being embarrassed in Tony's) that I'm siding with your friend… Or enemy, or whatever James is to you in that same stupid argument you've had with him for a hundred years. And I am—I am siding with James, because you're a whore, just like James has been more politely telling you for ages. You're such a whore, Carlton. You know, and I know, and everyone who sees you in the ads knows that you're a high-price trick saying whatever garbage that God-awful trade group tells you to say. You're a shill, Carlton. I'm ashamed of myself for sharing the money. I don't even need it. I'm not like the woman at home who depends on her man for every dollar. In fact, I could probably afford to live in our coveted ZIP Code without your nasty money."

She has seen his face change as she has spoken. The anger reached rage, then fell off, but at a tangent, into another realm entirely, centered on horror maybe. She processes as she talks, then addresses what she sees.

"Are you surprised, Carl? You look stricken. Even though I'm not too loud now, you're still stricken. You know why, Carl? Because your biggest fear's come true. Carl—you were right all along. You're not okay. You're not. You're a petty, self-absorbed, insecure little quivering man. You don't have a son, or a wife, or an oversized mausoleum for a house, nothing. Because you can only see Carl. I don't know when you got eyes only for yourself. I closed mine too for a long time. I didn't challenge it. I think I knew you were so breakable, and I didn't want to break you. Bad idea on my part, Carlton. You're more breakable than ever. You're hard, thin porcelain. I can't stop you from breaking any more."

She pauses when she sees the collecting of moisture at the bases of his eyes. For a moment, she feels sorry for him. She sees the young man, fragile but sweet. Talking even then with too much swagger, too much anger about the stupid views of others, about undeserved successes. The feeling sorry passes, though. She doesn't know if she has made some half-conscious effort to repulse feeling sorry, or if it's passed from her like so much else during this quick lunch.

"Carl, I'm going now. I have a lot to do before I go to Jason's conference. You remember Jason, don't you?" She feels, for the first time since she began, regret at being so mean. "Sorry, that's too much. But you really don't much remember him, Carl." She says this without snideness, with sadness. "You just can't. Or remember me. Or whatever it was you were or wanted to be. You can't remember, darling."

She pushes her chair back. He makes no move to wipe the tears from his face, no move of any kind by any part of his body. His eyes look down at the remnant of the sandwich.

She rises, lets her eyes scan the room to see if her disturbance still registers, sees mostly people back in their own lives, sees one woman smile, sees another look at her sharply. She knows the report won't get done on time, but no matter. There will be a time for amends, at least with her client.

Fiction

Tommy

LAWRENCE HELMS

These new glasses make me see better, a lot better. I'm not sure it's good to see better. A lot of stuff I see is sort of scary. When my mom and I got home with the new glasses, right off I spotted a new wasp nest by the garage door. I didn't see that one before. I don't know if it's better not to know about it or know about it. When I didn't know about it, like this morning, I didn't worry about being near it, but I could have got stung. Now I know about it, and I'm scared to go out the garage door, even though I usually do, but I might forget and still get stung anyway. So I don't know if I like these glasses or not. Also I see all those patterns in the rug with the roses more. They swirl and make all kinds of things come in my head and scare me.

I already know I'll have to be careful about how I take these glasses off when I go to bed and put them on the table by the lamp. Mom told me you don't sleep in them because you don't need them when you're asleep and they'd hurt your face and might break. She said it like I should've thought of it. I guess I should have. Soon as she said those things, they made sense. I've been try-ing not to ask so many questions. Aunt Louise looks like she likes to hear questions, even when Mom tells me to stop bothering Aunt Louise. Aunt Louise is very old and white and wrinkly all over her face, but she doesn't scare me. Maybe old people like questions more.

When I take off my glasses tonight, I know there's a perfect way to put them down on the table, but I don't know what it is yet. I never had anything I had to take off and put on the table before. But I have to do things just right, and I already know I'll have to do the glasses. I have to brush my teeth right, but I know how many times up and down and which side first and all. Sometimes I have to start over if my hand hits the sink or something when I put my toothbrush in the holder thing. But mostly I can do that right. So I know it will take a long time to put the glasses down right. I don't know what's right yet, and I'll have to learn it by trying.

I hope I can go to sleep. Sometimes I get stuck on things, like the prayers. I don't say them right, and I have to start over. Sometimes I get mad because I have to keep starting over, and then I get scared I won't go to sleep all night, and everybody else will be asleep before me, and that's the scariest, like that furnace down in the cellar. Sometimes I start crying. If my mom hears me, she comes in my room and asks me what is wrong. I like that, but I don't like it. I feel silly and sad. She already knows why I cry. I already told her lots of times it's because I didn't get my things right and I can't go to sleep and I'm scared I'll still be awake when it's quiet and dark and everybody is asleep and you can hear that furnace. Still, when she comes in, she asks me what's wrong. Every time. And I tell her again. She holds my hand and sometimes gives me a hug. But she doesn't make it stop. I don't know why she doesn't make it stop. Sometimes she says she'd do anything to make me feel better, but I don't know what she does. It doesn't help the things go away. Sometimes she looks tired, like she wants to go away and go back downstairs where the TV is. Sometimes she looks scared. That's the time I feel worse, and I might cry more. But so far, I go to sleep every time, even when it takes a long time. She always stays while I'm crying, and then I'm not sure if I'm crying because she stays or because I really have to cry. Sometimes she falls asleep in my room. I sort of like that.

My sisters make fun of me. They get mad and beat on the door of the bathroom if I have to do my steps washing my hands and brushing my teeth. Even when I'm peeing. They say I'm taking too long in there. Harriet says are you counting again but it's not a real question. She's just saying she knows I'm counting so I'll feel bad. But I already feel bad.

I think my dad knows I count and do steps. I think my mom told him. He never comes in when I cry. Sometimes he tells me to hurry up in there when my sisters get mad and bang on the door of the bathroom. Sometimes he tells me to hurry up even when my sisters don't. He has to shave and get ready for work. He was in a war and flew an airplane. I play war in the yard and pretend I fly it, too. But he never talks about the airplane. I wish he would. I wish he would tell me stories about it. But he doesn't. I heard my mom tell Aunt Louise he's a different man. I don't know what that means, but it makes me scared he isn't my dad, and he got switched some way in that war. He doesn't talk a lot, and he looks mad sometimes. He knows how to fix things and he's not scared. He goes in the cellar and works on the furnace even at night. I can't go down there at night.

My mom said the glasses will help me when I go to school next year. She said I couldn't see the board without them. I don't know what the board is, and I was about to ask her, but I remembered, and I stopped. I think I'll ask Harriet or Charlotte when they get home from school. But only if it looks like a nice day. Some days they are nice to me, and some they aren't. Sometimes they act nice, but I know it's because they want me to do something, like turn one end of the jump rope. If I have a game, they won't play it, even if I turn the rope. They're older than me and think I'm a baby, but I'm not. When I go to school, I'll be on the school bus with them. I don't like thinking about school. There are all those kids from town that know each other. Nobody lives near us but Aunt Louise and Uncle Silas in the big house. They're rich, and Uncle Silas is very important.

A boy came to our house with his dad one of the days before this one. I knew he was coming because my dad said Mr. Hodges was coming to talk about some work and he was bringing his boy. I had a plan for what we would do. I put some of my cars out, some for him and some for me. I gave him the bigger ones, because my dad said he's already in school. When he got there, he was bigger than I thought. I showed him the cars and the sand pile to make roads, but he didn't want to. He threw acorns at the old chicken coops and said he bet he could hit the roof and make a racket more than I could. I don't know how to throw good. My dad throws with me sometimes, but most of the time he mows the grass or fixes something or reads his books. The boy could throw real good and hit the roof almost every time. I only tried twice and missed, and he laughed. He played by himself the rest of the time. My dad said I didn't play much with Mr. Hodges' boy. He said it like I should have played with him more.

I don't even know why I'm talking about that boy. I don't remember his name. But it was just a few days ago, and I think my new glasses made me think how maybe I couldn't hit the roof because I couldn't see it good. Maybe that was why. I'd like to tell my dad that I think I need more practice throwing, but I'm scared to. Sometimes when he throws with me and I don't do good, he gets that look on his face that isn't very nice and shakes his head. But sometimes he says that's a little better. We had to stop last time because I missed the ball and it hit me on the lip. He said we better stop if I was going to get hurt like that. My mom made me put ice on my lip and made a bad face at dad.

But boy, I can see better. There's this little shed way down there in the field where Uncle Silas used to keep a horse. There's no horse there now. But I didn't even know there was a shed down there. I always see it from the driveway, but I thought it was a rock. That's sort of funny. But now I'm scared that other things are going to be something different than I thought they were. Like maybe I was even seeing some people wrong, or I thought they were people but they weren't. At least when I go to school I won't get surprised about what things are, because I've never seen them with my fuzzy eyes. That's what my mom called them, my fuzzy eyes. Today when we were coming home she said now I'm not fuzzy eyes, I'm four eyes. I don't know what that means, but I didn't want to ask. I think maybe I should know already.

Anyway, I'm not so sure about these glasses. Everything looks all straight and sort of alone, and they used to be sort of more together. I think I liked it better when they seemed sort of mixed up together, like they were friends or something. Now they look lonely. But I bet I'll get used to it. My mom said I'll get used to the glasses. I hope I do soon. I'll have to find just the right way to take them off and put them on the table. I know it will be hard, because I don't have the right way to do it yet. It won't seem right till I do it a lot of times. It might take me a long time, and I think I'll get scared that I'm the only one awake and might cry, and my mom will come in there and ask me why am I doing that thing with my glasses. And she might use that word she says for what I do. She calls it rituals. It sounds like a bad thing when she says it. But after I get it right the first time, I'll know how to do it other nights. But still, it takes the right steps to get it right even when you know exactly what is right.

Nonfiction

Why We Built the Lake House

JOHN J. JESSOP

We bought our waterfront lot on Smith Mountain Lake in 1982, when we had just turned 30, with a plan to build our lake house in 15 to 20 years. But they say life is what happens while you are making other plans, and life happened.

One Sunday morning in the spring of 1991, my wife and I were having coffee in the kitchen while the kids, Lizzy, 6, and Lilly, 3, were playing in the basement. I said, "Nancy, my commute is killing me, and Northern Virginia's getting more and more crowded every day. Herndon is turning into a smaller version of Los Angeles. My job is stressing me out, we never do anything fun, and being cooped up at home with the kids is driving me crazy. We need to get out of here for a while. I wish we could build a place on the lake, but we're just not ready yet. How about we take a short vacation? I was thinking we should try a camping trip."

She said, "I hear you, but do we really want to take the girls camping? It's hard enough to keep them corralled and safe in the house. And we don't know anything about camping. Where would we even go?"

But I was determined. I replied, "I desperately need to do something to break this cycle of stress, boredom, and raising two young daughters, and I'm also going through the beginnings of my first mid-life crisis. I'll look into places to camp within a reasonable distance of home. Meanwhile, I have a buddy at work who bought a long-wheelbase, Ford panel van and had it converted into a camper. He found a place in Maryland that'll do the conversion at a reasonable price."

Nancy gave me the eye roll with the nonverbal message, "You've lost another marble." She followed with, "Are you kidding? Please tell me you're kidding. You always go all-in on everything. Now, you want to go camping, but we can't just take tents like normal people. You have to buy a van and pay someone to convert it into a camper? How are we going to afford it? We're struggling to save money to build a lake house, we don't want another loan, and we agreed not to build until we have enough to pay cash."

I just smiled knowingly, "Calm down, Honey, and trust me. We can start out by camping close to home, and if that works out we can eventually drive to the lake on weekends and camp on our lot until we have the funds to build. I'll get on the van thing right away."

"Okay. I'll go camping with you, if you manage to come up with a converted van and find a reasonable place to camp. I guess the girls would probably enjoy it. So, all right, let's do this. Let's go camping," she said somewhat reluctantly.

I knew she didn't believe I'd follow through with my grand plan and just agreed with me to shut me up. To her surprise, a month later, I drove home in a brand-new, long-wheelbase, Ford panel van, converted into a camper. I called Nancy and the girls outside to give them the tour of our new home on wheels. My wife took a seat on the strange looking couch that served as a rear seat. I told her, "The van has been modified for camping, with paneling, carpet, and a back seat that automatically re-adjusts itself into a comfortable bed at the push of a button." I reached out and pushed a red button on the side of the couch thing, and it began automatically to unfold itself into a bed, carrying my wife along with it.

Nancy screeched, "What the hell are you doing? Are you trying to kill me?"

I said, "Stay cool, woman. Just go with the flow. I want you to see how comfortable the bed is."

The girls laughed, watching their mom slowly recline as the couch automatically flattened into a bed. Lizzy said, "Mommy has to put a quarter in the cuss jar."

I continued to show them the finer points of the conversion

van. "See here? They also included space for a modified crib for Lilly at the foot of the bed, and floor space for a sleeping bag for Lizzy. I had them modify a crib for Lilly because at her age she's so active that I figured we needed bars to contain her."

Lizzy interrupted, "Lilly's gonna sleep in a baby crib? What do you think about that, little one? You're still a baby."

Lilly cried, "Shut up, Lizzy. I am not a baby."

I continued, "The front windows have been fitted with screens and a small fan for proper ventilation. We'll all be very comfortable in here, nice and cozy together."

Nancy said, "Isn't this thing too small for the four of us? You're six feet seven inches tall. How are you going to sleep on this bed? There won't be any room for me. We can't live in here for an entire weekend. We'll go crazy."

"We're just going to sleep in the van," I replied. "We'll have a large screened tent for a kitchen, another one for a living area in case it rains, and the entire outdoors as our playroom."

Nancy said, exasperated, "Judging from the size of you and this bed, you might end up in one of the tents, or the playroom. And just how much did this monstrosity cost? When we talked about this, I didn't think you'd actually go through with it. I just agreed to shut you up. I should've known better. Now we're actually going to go camping, in the woods, with the bugs, and snakes, and bears."

Lizzy said, "Bugs, and snakes, and bears? We're gonna die!"

Lilly said, "Mommy. I don't wanna die!"

I said, "No worries, my children. Daddy will protect you. I am much man. I ain't afraid of no bears. I'll just wrestle that old bear to the ground and bite off his ear. That ought to chase him away."

Nancy just rolled her eyes and said, "Hot damn, I feel better already. Perhaps I should increase much man's life insurance before this trip."

Lizzy said, "Mommy has to put a quarter in the cuss jar. And Daddy, don't hurt the poor bear. That's not nice."

A couple of weeks later, in early May, we decided to do a trial run. I had them all corralled in the kitchen, and I announced, "Next weekend is a four-day one, and I made reservations for a campsite at a small place just outside Front Royal, called Land of Lakes State Park. It's only about an hour and a half away, and if things don't go well, we can easily flee back to the comforts of home. But what could possibly go wrong on a simple camping trip?"

Nancy rolled her eyes and said, "Yeah. What could possibly go wrong?"

We loaded up two large tents, food, and clothing for a two-night trip and headed out Thursday after work. We arrived at the park around seven that evening, just an hour before dusk. It had started raining lightly about half an hour into the trip, and the wife and I were already beginning to get a bad feeling. I spoke up first, false hope in my voice, "No worries, it's just a light rain. It'll cool things down, keep the bugs away, and tomorrow will be a beautiful day."

Nancy looked at the girls in the back seat and said, "Yeah. No worries. We're gonna have a great time. We'll toast marshmallows, and your father will protect us from the bears and stuff."

The girls' eyes got really big, and Lilly said, "I'm scared of bears."

Lizzy said, "Mom, there are no bears around here. Are there? Dad was just kidding, right?"

Lilly cried, "Daddy said there are bears and he will protect us."

Nancy said, "Don't worry. Your father will protect us. Won't you, Dear?"

I said, "Who's gonna protect me?"

Nancy said, "You promised to wrestle any bears to the ground and bite off their ears. And, by the way, for your information, I did increase your life insurance policy to a cool million, so wrestle all the bears you want."

I just sighed and kept on driving.

As we drove through the park towards our assigned campsite, Nancy said, "Oh, look, Dear, Land of Lakes State Park does, in-deed, have three man-made lakes. Or, more accurately, there's a very small man-made lake, and two man-made mud puddles. Only one of the lakes has actually been filled with water. But, the good news is, if it keeps raining, maybe the other two will fill up, too."

I flinched at her barb as I started to back the van onto our campsite. It consisted of a raised gravel platform with a retaining wall on the lake side. I said, "At least our campsite is located on the lake that actually contains water. Could you please get out and guide me so I don't back over the retaining wall, through that small patch of evergreens, and into the lake."

My wife got out and walked around to the back of the van, stationing herself so that I could see her in my side mirror. She said, "Straight back now, slowly, slowly. Just a little more. Stop! You really don't want to put this thing in the lake. I'm betting your fine conversion van won't float, and our daughters are still inside."

I said, "I'm inside, too. What about me? Don't you care if I sink to the bottom of the lake?"

She just laughed and said, "Sink to the bottom? You could stand up in the middle of this so-called lake, and your head would be entirely out of the water."

Once I had set the emergency brake, the girls jumped out, and my wife and I began to unload the tents and set up camp in the light rain. It took well over an hour for us to finish. By then it was almost dark, and we were both soaking wet. I said, shaking my head to fling the rain out of my drenched hair, "See, that wasn't so bad. And now we're all ready for a good night's sleep."

Nancy responded, "But, Dear, we haven't had dinner yet. I'll fire up the gas stove and boil us up some hot dogs. Meanwhile, why don't you round up the girls and do campsite things with them?"

The rain had subsided for the moment, and Lizzy and Lilly had disappeared. I said to my wife, "I don't see the girls. Where the hell are they? I hope they didn't wander down by the lake. They don't have on life jackets, and Lilly can't swim yet. I better look for them." I yelled in the direction of the so-called lake, "Hey monkeys, where are you? Are you okay?" I said to Nancy, "I'm going to go find the girls. I'll be right...Aaaah! Shiiiit! Umph!" As I jumped off the end of the retaining wall, I didn't consider the fact that it had been raining, and when my feet hit the ground, I slipped in the mud and fell hard on my butt. I tried to lessen the impact with my hands, resulting in a sore rear end and muddy hands. In spite of the pain, I was very worried about the girls, so I bounced right back up and continued on toward the water's edge. I yelled to my wife, "I'm okay. I'm not dead yet. Stupid rain!"

When I broke through the trees, I didn't know how to respond to what I saw. Lizzy and Lilly were sitting on a log, several yards from the water's edge, and Lizzy was laughing hysterically. Lilly's clothes were in a pile on the ground, and her body was the bright blue color of a Smurf. The girls had gotten bored with mom and dad setting up the tents, and Lizzy had taken some chalk from her drawing kit, collected muddy water from the lake, mixed up a bright blue concoction in a plastic toy bucket, and used it to paint her younger sister, head to toe. My tiny daughter, all blue with her shiny blonde hair, looked just like Smurfette. As I showed up, Lilly started crying, and I couldn't tell if it was from chalk in her eyes, the fact that she was cold, or the fact that her sister was laughing at her.

"What did you do?" I bellowed at my older daughter. "Are you crazy?" To Lilly I said, "Are you okay, little one? Your sister has lost her mind, and there will be consequences. Let's get that stuff off of you and get you into some warm clothes." To Lizzy I said, "Daughter, go to your room...I mean, go to the van. You're banished to the van until I figure out your punishment."

It took a while, but I finally got Lilly washed clean of the liquid chalk and dressed in warm, dry clothes. Meanwhile, Nancy had finished fixing hot dogs and beans, and she yelled, "Soup's on. Come and get it. Come on, girls, the hot dogs are getting cold." Lizzy's punishment had consisted of sitting in the van watching a movie on her portable VHS player, but I was too tired to push it any further.

By the time we finished dinner, it was nine o'clock and raining again. The girls were all wound up, and the kitchen tent simply wasn't big enough for the four of us. The wife and I were sitting, drinking coffee, and the two girls were as far to the other end of the tent as possible, looking at books. I looked up and said, "Oh crap, where's Lilly? Lizzy, do you know where your sister went?"

Lizzy said, "I think she just sneaked out of the tent."

Then we heard a crash, followed by crying. "Aaaaah! Bleeding. I hurt myself!"

I, being the protector, jumped up and fearlessly ran out into the rain to rescue my younger daughter. I yelled to my wife, "She's okay. She fell off the retaining wall and landed on her hands and knees. Her pants are torn, her knee and one hand are scratched up, and she's muddy from head to toe, but she's okay."

I carried Lilly into the tent, and Nancy cleaned her up and bandaged her knee. At that point I was exhausted. I said, "Okay, monkeys. Let's all go to bed. Mom will take you to the restroom, where you can shower and brush your teeth, and then it's off to bed for the night. We'll get a good night's sleep and start fresh in the morning. I'm sure the rain will let up by then."

After the usual arguing and grumbling, my wife managed to herd the girls off to the campsite facilities. When they returned, Nancy said, "The bathrooms are disgusting. Next time, pick a better place to camp."

At that point, I had the van set up for the night. I said, "Okay, girls. Lizzy, snuggle down into your nice warm, comfy sleeping bag. I'll put Lilly into her crib thing, and we can all go to sleep." With that, I picked Lilly up and placed her in the converted crib. "Good night, Lilly. We love you."

Nancy and I got comfortable on the fold-down bed. Lizzy was surprisingly quiet, tired from the hard work of painting her little sister blue. After some shuffling around in the converted crib, Lilly seemed to quiet down, too. Lying on my back and listening to the relaxing downpour of rain on the van roof, I had just nodded off into a pleasant and sorely needed sleep, when I felt a sharp pain in my groin, followed by pressure on my upper torso as Lilly crawled up my body, placed her face just above mine, looked me in the eyes, and said in a wide awake voice, "Hi Daddy."

Nancy and I both laughed when we realized what had happened. I took her in my arms, placed her back in her crib, and said, "Come on now, Lilly, it's bedtime. Time to go to sleep. You need to stay in your cage...I mean bed."

But Lilly wasn't having any of that. She was wide awake, and time after time, all through the night, she kept escaping the crib, climbing up onto my body, never once missing the chance to plant a foot or knee in my groin, and then looking me square in the face and saying, quite emphatically, "Hi Daddy." This went on until six in the morning, and my wife and I got no sleep at all.

Completely exhausted, I said, "Nancy, I wish we'd have thought to bring something to put over the top of that crib thing. Four walls just aren't enough. We need a full-blown cage."

So, at six o'clock on Friday morning with no sleep, we decided to get up and fix breakfast. When I looked out the window, it was starting to get light outside, and a heavy cloud-cover still hung over the campgrounds. Just as I opened the side door of the van and stepped out, on my way to the bathroom, the sky opened up, and it felt like someone was dumping bathtubs full of water on my head. I was drenched from head to toe. To no one in particular I bellowed, "Damn camping! Damn rain! Whose stupid idea was this, anyhow? You gotta have a screw loose to leave the warm, dry comfort of your home for this!" With that said, I slipped and fell on my face in the mud. "Craaaap!"

Liiy said, "Daddy has to put a quarter in the cuss jar."

The bathroom was damp and filthy; at least one toilet was clogged, and the odor of human waste hung in the air. I looked around and said to no one in particular, "This is nice. The showers look like they've never been cleaned, the green mold covering the shower curtains is most attractive, and the musty smell is almost as bad as the toilets." I relieved myself and then noticed there was no soap or paper towels. I was afraid to wash my hands in the grimy sink. I wiped my hands and face on my shirt sleeves and fled back to the van.

When I got back from the bathroom, Nancy was sitting on the bed with her hands over her ears. Both girls were yelling at once. Lilly was crying, wailing above the noise of the storm. Lizzy was screaming that she was cold and hungry and wanted to go home. My wife looked like she was going to strangle me, then jump out of the van, and run away. Standing there, looking at my distraught family through the side door of the van, I made a command decision. I ordered, "Family. We're getting the hell out of here. Wife, let's pack up and head home." I looked at Lilly and said, "I know, another quarter for the cuss jar."

In the pouring and blowing rain, I walked to the back of the van, frantically yanked down the two large, soaking-wet tents, wadded them up, and threw tents, stakes, clean and dirty kitchen equipment, the whole lot, into the back. Then I told my wife, "Nancy, push the button to convert the bed back into a bench seat, buckle everyone in, and let's get the hell out of Dodge." For once, no one argued with me.

We made good time getting home, and the girls slept the entire trip. Next morning, over lots of coffee, my wife and I had a brief conversation. She said, "Well, that was fun. Camping sucks."

"I tend to agree," I responded. "But the good news is, I think it's time to build the lake house. It'd be like camping in the woods, but in a nice, warm, dry, comfortable house, with real beds, and the children way up the hall in their own rooms. That needs to be a key point in the house design."

To my surprise, she said, "I agree one hundred percent. So what if we have to take out a loan to build? Better than strangling each other. We should start looking at lake house plans tomorrow."

And, that was that for family camping. Life had happened and nudged us in a different direction. The van appeared for sale in the want-adds the very next week. We still wanted to escape the stress and crowds of Northern Virginia, camping sucked, and it was time to build our lake house. It was completed in 1992, the very next year.

Nonfiction

New Jersey in an Exotic New Car

JOHN KETWIG

After returning from the wars in Southeast Asia, I found a job as a car salesman for a Volvo, Triumph, Jaguar, Lotus, Saab, and Fiat dealership in Rochester, New York. One summer afternoon I ventured outside to meet a customer. He was surprisingly eager to buy a new Volvo model he had seen written-up in a car enthusiast magazine. He and his wife were well-dressed young professionals and eager to get right to the point. He wanted to buy a Volvo 142-E, a brand-new, special-edition two-door with Volvo's first fuel-injected engine, leather seats, and special metallic paint. My boss phoned Volvo and was assured that the first cars were on a ship headed for the port at Newark, New Jersey. We could reserve one and, because the customer was so eager, fly down to Newark and drive it back. The customer agreed to buy the car with a few hundred miles on the odometer, added a list of accessories, and wrote a check. Within a few days I was on a plane to exotic Newark. Clutching a briefcase containing a dealer (license) plate, some necessary paperwork, a tattered copy of *Car and Driver* magazine, a map of New York State, and directions to the port facility, I found a taxi and showed the driver the address, feeling very, very important.

A few minutes later we were at Volvo's Newark port terminal, surrounded by a vast sea of imported cars in neat rows. I had arrived, in more ways than one! I paid the cab driver, included a generous tip, and entered the trailer that served as an office. I had sold a car, and now I was here in exotic New Jersey, entrusted to drive the prize vehicle back to Rochester, a valued representative of my company!

The 142-E was brand new, so new that dealers had only seen spec sheets. This was the first shipment, only seven cars, and I would take one home and deliver it to its new owner, long before most dealers would ever see their first one. The metallic paint was stunning, and the leather seats were plush under the thick plastic sheeting that protected them. Truly, this was a grand-touring sedan, a splendid performance-oriented highway car with power and road manners that had the enthusiast magazines raving. The 142-E signaled a bold new direction in upscale family sedans, a Swedish benchmark for all luxury road cars. Since it docked two days before, the car had been made drivable, the windshield cleared of stickers, and the tank gassed. The paperwork took only a few minutes. I checked the map, discussed my route with the people in the trailer, attached the dealer tag to the rear of the Volvo, and donned my sunglasses. The engine purred to life, and I glanced at the map one more time and drove away into New Jersey traffic, north on Interstate 95 alongside the Hudson River, with the amazing skyline of New York City on my right.

I took exit 16W toward the Sports Complex and passed the stadium where the Giants and the Jets play football. Just a little farther on I went north on Route 17, a busy but narrow highway. I would go about fifteen miles and get onto the New York State Thruway, and in a few hours I would be home. I sat back, loosened my collar, and gloated as the Volvo attracted a great deal of attention. I hadn't sold many cars. I was new to the business, young and enthusiastic, and this was my best deal ever! The customer had paid sticker price, even for the accessories. I would make a good commission on this car, and there was the extra bonus of this trip, the honor of being one of the very first people in America to drive a Volvo 142-E on public streets and highways. I knew people were noticing. Informed people, car enthusiasts like myself. A Volvo driver had even given me a thumbs-up a few minutes ago! My smile filled the windshield.

I was headed north on Route 17, a crowded retail thorough-fare, looking for the Garden State Parkway that would take me to the New York State Thruway. Route 17 had changed its look as I made my way north. The narrow road had expanded to four lanes each way, and now a battered sign indicated that I was in Paramus. The guy at the port trailer had joked that Paramus was an old Indian word meaning "Land of the Shopping Malls." Four lanes each way now, at seventy miles an hour, and the drivers entered and exited or changed lanes with a crazy carelessness. There was heavy construction too, all along the right shoulder. Orange and white striped reflective barrels, a myriad of signs. Cement trucks and backhoes, heavy equipment, workmen in hard hats and fluorescent vests, barriers. A maelstrom of activity. I had a way to go, so I maneuvered into the left lane and tried to relax.

The road curved left and under a series of overpasses, and as I came out into the bright sunlight I looked up toward another highway and saw a huge sign with the familiar New York State Thruway logo and an arrow indicating that my destination was off to my right. Access to it was quickly disappearing behind me! Should I have turned somewhere? Surely I hadn't traveled anything near fifteen miles, but the sign had been unmistakable.

I panicked. I needed to ask directions. I moved the Volvo right a lane, and then another. Now cars were darting in and out like bees around a hive, and their pace increased even as I tried to slow and determine where I should go. I dodged a truck and got into the second lane, then braked hard to get into the far-right lane. The construction was maddening, too many signs were zipping past, and the other drivers were nuts! I had traveled more than a mile past the overpass, and I was getting very concerned. Then I saw a gas station with a broad entrance and a huge temporary sign that read "THIS WAY TO ERNIE'S SHELL." There was a bold red arrow, an invitation that guided me into their driveway. I glanced at the mirror and slowed abruptly and guided the wonderful car into the entrance...

CRASH!

Confused, panicking, I knew only that I had hit something,

that I was falling hard against the seatbelt and toward the steering wheel, but I couldn't see any twisted or damaged sheet metal. Disoriented, shaken, there was nothing to do but get out. The engine had stalled, all manner of red and yellow lights were blinking across the dashboard, and I didn't have time to determine what they all meant. I shut off the key to quiet the display. I had to get out, so I released the belt and unlatched the door. The bulky Swedish door was very heavy and difficult to open. To my left a burly man in a yellow hard hat was running toward me and shouting, cursing, and waving his arms. His face was red, and his language was blue!

I squeezed out of the door, a feat in itself. I had emerged into bright sun, and the man was nearly upon me. "You idiot!" he screamed, then added a string of the obscenities that are considered polite greetings in New Jersey traffic. I stepped away from the car and looked at the situation. The car's position was surreal, tilted far forward, the entire front from the windshield forward having disappeared into a deep gray puddle. Now the guy was grabbing my arm and shouting wildly. I raised my left arm to protect myself and cocked my right, but the guy didn't seem interested in hurting me. What the hell was happening?

"We've got to get it out! I mean, we've got to get it out right away!" The man was frantic. I was very seriously confused, and I stepped back a little more and forced my eyes to focus. I was able to comprehend that the front of the car had fallen into a huge, gray puddle. How had that happened? The man was tugging at my sleeve again, frenzied, and screaming. "What the #&@* were you thinking?"

I was stunned, dazed. I pointed to the huge sign just a few feet to the left that read, "THIS WAY TO ERNIE'S SHELL."

"Oh, damn!" the man cried, his voice bloated with despair and disbelief. "I told the kid to move that sign this morning." He stumbled away, seething, to measure the situation, and then returned. In those brief moments, I had re-evaluated the predicament and determined that the beautiful Volvo 142-E sedan had fallen head-first into a huge trough of wet cement! At this moment it was imitating the Titanic, tail up, its frame resting on the pavement, and the pond of cement extending almost to the windshield posts!

"We've got to get it out," the guy was ranting, "before that stuff sets up! In a few minutes your car will be a permanent part of the landscape, buddy!"

Ernie, the owner of the Shell station, and his staff had heard the crash, and now they approached with a huge tow truck. Ernie was a heavyset Italian guy with bushy eyebrows and a dirty T-shirt. He climbed down out of the truck, appraised the situation, and announced that they would have to haul the car out backwards... which would require that traffic be stopped on Route 17! As if he had heard Ernie's thinking, a New Jersey State Trooper approached up the shoulder, lights flashing and siren screaming. After an eternity spent checking my license and the car's dealer registration, he conferred with Ernie, then agreed that traffic would have to be halted.

Ernie leapt into the wrecker, and the officer approached the jostling traffic with his hand upraised. Of course, a lot of New Jersey drivers accelerated to get away before the big delay that would certainly result, many of them raising their hands in a favorite New Jersey salute as they squeezed past. Finally, however, the entire northbound Route 17 ground to a halt, all five lanes, although the drivers continued to holler, gesture, and blow their horns. Ernie drove out of the other exit from his lot and maneuvered the giant truck behind the beached Volvo. He leapt from the cab, got down on his knees to attach chains to the car's undercarriage, and, returning to the rear of his truck, hauled at the control levers.

The chains began to tighten. The car shuddered, wanting to escape this mess, but then the giant wrecker's front wheels began to lift off the ground! Ernie released the tension, and the huge truck settled back to earth. Ernie shouted instructions, and an employee sprinted into the gas station. Within moments the man appeared, awkwardly hauling heavy chains across the pavement, up and out the exit and down the shoulder to the front of the tow truck. The trooper was holding traffic at bay with his upraised hand, but the horns and catcalls were a threatening din. Without speaking, Ernie met his guy, and they stretched the chains from the truck's front axle to the upright posts supporting the guardrail out on the grassy median.

Ernie returned to his control levers. The engine strained and the chains tightened. The nose of the wrecker threatened to lift again and then froze, and the Volvo began to inch backward. The huge truck groaned and squatted, but finally the Volvo's front wheels came free and up out of the muck onto *terra firma*, and immediately the honking and shouting from the audience increased. The assistant got into the car as soon as it was feasible. Surprisingly, he got the Volvo to start. He drove it gingerly down the shoulder, into the Shell station's exit, and up close to the building's plate glass office. The policeman stood his ground, Ernie gathered up his chains and maneuvered the giant truck out of the way, the construction guys attempted to clear the highway with push brooms that were clearly never intended to push concrete, and traffic was set free to flow again. The delayed drivers took pains to express their observations and opinions as they began to resume their travels, but the backup eventually cleared. The guys in the yellow hard hats were animated as they discussed how to smooth out the pool and fill in the impression of a Volvo front end that had disturbed their artwork. And all the while, no one moved the sign!

My proud new car was a huge rolling lump of wet gray goo. I was frantic, far from home, with my ride slowly turning into a brick. I finally got the garage owner's attention, and he produced a water hose and a brush. "You've gotta get that stuff off soon!" he announced, supremely confident in the authority bestowed by the yellow Shell logo embroidered on the chest of his uniform shirt.

It took about two hours to clean the car. Miraculously, there didn't seem to be any body damage, and I was able to wash the gritty coating off most of the mechanicals under the hood. The fenders and grille were difficult, and the wheels and brake mechanisms were just about impossible to clean. Finally, however, I tried a couple of mini test-runs across the station's parking lot and felt confident that I could continue my journey. Recalling how I had originally gotten into this mess, I summoned Ernie and discussed the best route to the New York State Thruway. Ernie, to my great surprise, began to write up a bill.

We discussed it for a while, and with high emotions. The construction guy agreed to pay for the wrecker service, but I had to whack my credit card for fifty dollars-worth of water Ernie estimated the cleanup had consumed! Of course, the cement that I washed off the Volvo was lying on the gas station's parking lot like residue, and he made me push it off into the weeds, then hose down his asphalt. It was late afternoon before I was ready to leave. I bothered Ernie for change to use the pay phone and call work to tell them I would be late. They were not amused when I explained why.

I was hungry, wet, and tired when I finally steered the Volvo out of Ernie's Shell. To my great surprise, the car performed perfectly all the way home. The mechanics went over it very carefully, cleaning everything, and when it was cleaned up and made ready for delivery, the car looked terrific. There was no visible damage, and the customer was never informed of the bizarre incident. He drove the car with great pride and pleasure for a number of years and never experienced any problem. My automotive career had just begun with that very memorable transaction.

Fiction

The Bad Seed

CHUCK LUMPKIN

My Journey - The Beginning

I was in one hell of a predicament. My ship was limping along with one engine blasted to pieces, the long-range scanner array gone, and the one remaining rail gun very low on ammunition. And if that wasn't bad enough, I'd run out of peanuts. The bad guys were winning this battle. If I wasn't careful, I'd end up part of the debris scattered around this planet.

I selected the super-secret subspace frequency for the Easties command center and announced "This is the Liberator. I am in-bound and being fired on by both sides. I have your cargo. I have one engine out and need assistance to make it to the spaceport." I flipped off the com and waited. It took only an instant.

"Liberator, please press your ID key for authentication." I pressed the ID key. "ID received and approved for insertion into orbit for landing. Can you maneuver well enough to land?"

I examined all the displays. "Command, this is the Libera-tor. I'm not sure I can handle the landing procedure manually. I'll switch to AutoNav and attempt. Please have the port stand by for immediate cargo transfer or a huge clean up detail." I had an idea what the cargo was but really didn't care.

"Liberator, you are cleared for landing. Good luck, buddy."

I managed to bring up the aft-view screen to observe if I was going to hit the surface at some unmanageable speed and end up like a squashed insect. The clouds were too thick to see.

The screen began to clear. I could see a huge complex directly below. The shaking and noise were mind-numbing. I'd no idea how fast I was going or if I'd crash.

As if I willed them, the retro rockets fired. I was pushed back into my seat with at last 3 Gs. I was surprised when the main engine stopped. I felt the bump of the landing pods hitting the pad. All was dead quiet. My whole body was trembling badly, and I was having trouble releasing the safety harness.

With a shaking finger I managed to press the cargo hatch button. Within minutes the cargo was out and off to wherever. I was pretty sure the cargo was plasma for the Easties weapons. I sat very still for several minutes and thought about how close this had been. I pressed the com button. "Uh, I need to talk to someone about the damage to my ship."

"You may disembark and go to the general command office. Ask for General Roman's office. The general will be expecting you." I needed a shower, so I decided to go to the hotel first.

The ramp to the ship's entrance hatch was already in place. I opened the hatch and walked down to the arrivals hall. A young officer looked at me with a strange expression. "Were you in the battle? Your landing was broadcast on the national feed. I've never seen a landing at that speed."

"It was broadcast?" Oh crap. The kid looked at me with awe and motioned for me to proceed to the exit.

I checked into a hotel and slept for ten hours. My com unit buzzed and woke me. It was April, my agent. We agreed to meet for dinner that night at the hotel. I thought about my ship and what was being done to repair it. I called the General's office and was told the ship had been moved to the shipyard for repairs. It was going to take two weeks to repair all the damage.

***

I met April in the hotel's lounge.

"Hi. It's been sort of hectic for the last couple of days," I said. She looked directly in my eyes. Damn, they disturbed me, in a good way. I tingled all the way to my toes.

"I contacted the general and added some components to your ship." April flashed me a smile.

"Components! What kind of components?"

"I suggested that a new warp manifold would be beneficial to all so you could double your warp speed. The manifold is not exactly new, but it will give you warp 4.0, twice as fast as your current drive."

"Wow, that's great. We can get twice as much cargo delivered in the same time. Business looks good." I was amazed at April. She had more angles than a crystal. We ordered dinner and discussed future business. "With the defeat of the Westies, do you think the Easties will still want more cargo?"

She hesitated for a second. "I've been thinking about that. When I spoke to the general, I asked. She said at least two more shipments should complete their need. So I started looking around for something with a lower profile. I think I have found just the thing and at a much higher fee."

"Higher fee? How illegal is this going to be?"

"Totally legal. In fact, you'll be doing some long-range runs with very legal cargo. The client monitors the seeding of planets by the Alliance. They are what you might call a watchdog group and are known as the Treme`."

"You said long-range runs. How long range?"

"With your new warp manifold, I'd say you can make the round trip in two weeks. The job is on New Earth."

"New Earth! I've heard of that seeding project. That system is on the other side of the galaxy. Are you sure the fee is high enough?"

"The fee is twenty bars of pure Latium for each run. The load is time sensitive, so the new warp manifold is essential to the job."

"Twenty bars? Holy crap! Do you know what the cargo will be?"

"No, but I was told that it is an essential part of the seeding program. When will your ship be repaired?"

"The general said two weeks, but that was just a guess. I hope your enhancements won't prolong the repairs."

The Liberator was ready in ten days. Not only had a new warp manifold been installed, but two new rail guns and four missile-launch tubes with a compliment of twelve missiles and enough rail-gun ammo to stand off a battleship. I made the last two runs back to Sparta Prime for the Easties in record time and was paid in full. I was on my way to meet my new client on New Earth.

***

New Earth came in view. The scanners showed large oceans and land masses. I sat and watched as the AutoNav made course adjustments and began the approach. The ship entered the atmosphere and began to slow for landing. I could not see a spaceport. The ship appeared to be heading directly for a huge rock in a desert.

The ship slowed to almost standstill speed. Two large doors opened, and the ship dropped down below the surface. I had never landed below the surface before. The AutoNav unit announced "You have arrived at your destination. Route guidance will now cease." In three thousand years, they have not come up with a better announcement, and the voice was the same female.

The com unit beeped. "Liberator, you will be berthed at T-09." I felt the ship move. We were on some sort of device that moved the ship to a berthing area. Soon the movement ceased. "Liberator, the ramp has been attached. You are cleared to disembark. Welcome to New Earth."

I entered the arrivals hall and approached the credentials desk. The officer looked up at me and pressed a button that updated my credentials pad. I headed toward the exit and entered a large lobby with rows and rows of elevators. A sign over one of the elevators read "Accommodations."

I was surprised that the actual hotel was far down below the spaceport. I went to the front desk and got my key-card. The condo was large, with two sleeping chambers, a small office area, and a large main room. There was even a kitchen.

The condo's com buzzed. I answered, "This is Steve."

"Hi, Steve. Welcome to New Earth. I'm Andra. I will be your contact and will send you instructions for our cargo. We will not meet at this time. There will also be contact information that is very important. Please read over all the instructions. Welcome to New Earth." The connection broke. How did she know I had checked in?

About an hour later, the com unit buzzed again. Now what? A female voice told me she was with the spaceport police and there were some unauthorized personnel attempting to get into my ship. All of the police were involved in another matter, and I should go to the berth area and secure my ship.

I was alarmed, of course. All of my Latium stash was on the ship. I rushed into the sleeping chamber and grabbed the blaster from my flight bag. I was in a panic. I ran to the elevators and pressed the launch bay level button.

I ran to the berth area. I saw someone going up the ramp. The person turned, and laser beams began flying in every direction. I took cover behind a large mobile machine. I raised and fired at the individual on the ramp. The figure fell and rolled off to the surface below. I ran up the ramp and tried to enter the code to open the hatch. When I stuck my left hand up to the pad, I felt searing pain. I ducked back down and looked at my burned hand.

Black particles from blaster hits covered the front of my tunic, and the smell of burned flesh filled my nostrils. My left hand throbbed. Oh crap, here came two more wise-asses. The noise was deafening. I took aim at the two intruders and shot both before they reached the top of the ramp. I decided to get off the ramp to the main hatch and drop down to the airlock hatch.

I thrust my blaster into its holster. With my right hand I punched in the code on the pad for the airlock. More blaster beams as bright as the sun were hitting all around me. The stupid hatch was taking forever to open. I jerked my blaster from its holster in preparation for another assault as the hatch swung open. No more blaster beams came.

I went to my quarters on the ship and nursed my hand. It was beginning to hurt badly. I gave myself an injection of MaxPlus, a combo-injection of pain killers and antibiotics. I fell onto my bed. I slept soundly for 7 hours and was dreaming of April when the sound of beeping woke me. I couldn't figure out was happening. I rolled out of the bunk and ran to the bridge. The ship's com unit was beeping loud enough to wake the dead. "This is the Liberator."

"Liberator, this is Spaceport control. Are you okay?" The voice sounded vaguely familiar.

I looked at the com unit for a few seconds, then spoke. "Yes, I'm okay. I slept on the ship last night. I had a little problem getting into the ship, as there were several armed individuals who were not so keen on my survival."

The control agent replied, "We have noted from the security recordings that you were attacked. It appears you ran the intruders off. We found no bodies at the ramp, although we saw that you had hit at least three before you entered your ship. They must have taken their wounded or dead with them."

"Yeah, well, that's something I will leave for you to figure out. I was hit in the hand, but nothing too serious. Are there any protocols I should be aware of that will prevent me from leaving and returning?" I was concerned about having the weapon. She didn't ask why I was armed, which I thought was odd.

"No, we are satisfied that you handled the situation fine. All you need to do is file a launch plan with the date and time you wish to depart, and all will be arranged."

***

I examined the ship's com unit. To my surprise there was a setting for Hypervista. I contacted the client using the old frequency system they recommended. I turned the dial to the proper frequency and pressed the announce button.

"Yes Steve, what can I do for you?" She sounded a lot like the Spaceport officer who spoke to me earlier. Maybe she worked for both.

"May I speak with Andra?" Andra came on immediately. "Andra, I ran into a bit of a problem last night. Some bad guys attempted to steal my ship."

"I'm sorry to hear that. Maybe you should give the cargo run a test. I will send you the coordinates for the pickup and file a launch plan for you. You should prepare to leave in about two hours. Have a safe trip."

Wow, she sounded like she wanted me off the planet in a hurry. I thanked her and disconnected. There were some strange things going on, but I didn't know what.

I put on my flight gear. There was nothing at the condo that I needed. As the launch timer ticked down I checked all the instruments. Everything was ready.

The AutoNav launched the ship and engaged the warp-drive. The ship went smoothly to warp 4.0. I sat back with a sigh of relief. I had stocked up on peanuts. My first run for the new client was underway.

About thirty minutes later, the ship gave a shudder. A warning blared from the alarm systems. The ship shook violently for several minutes as the warp drive shut down. The navigation system indicated I had traveled 7.2 light years from the solar system. The computer indicated that the warp drive was shagged. I'd have to do with subwarp speeds.

I thought about April. It'd been a long time since April and I had hooked up. I pressed her number on the sub-space com panel. "April! April! Answer up!"

For several seconds, only static came out of the com unit, then April's voice boomed out of the panel. "Steve Gibson! Bloody hell, you scared the crap out of me. Don't you ever send an alert announcement before connecting?"

"April, we need to talk. I've had an attack on my ship. Some dudes tried to steal the ship, and I'm wounded."

There was silence, then "How bad is the wound?"

"It's my left hand. I got shot trying to get into the ship. It's reparable and will be good as new in a few weeks. I'm on my way to our client's pickup point. The warp drive went down. I need that manifold fixed. Please help me."

"Maybe. Tell me exactly what happened?"

I told her the whole story.

"Where are you now?"

"The AutoNav says I made it 7.2 light years from New Earth's solar system. A short stop at Sparta Prime will not affect the delivery. I'm guessing it'll take about a week. I have at least 1 week's grace on the delivery."

"I'll look around and see if I can locate a new warp manifold. It'll cost a lot."

"Fine. I'll check in tomorrow with a better estimate of arrival. Bye for now." The com went dead.

I was exhausted, and my mind wandered. I experienced a feeling of complete relaxation from the MaxPlus shot and was very sleepy.

Intruder

I felt the ship rock slightly. My eyes popped open. I had fallen asleep on the bridge. The panel for the cargo bay external doors indicated the doors were opening. The environmental system's verbal alarm shouted "Warning, Warning A space vacuum now exists in the cargo hold. All access ports will be sealed."

Oh crap, now what? I switched on the view panel for the cargo hold. Sitting in the middle of the cargo hold was a shuttle craft of unknown origin. I pressed the containment field button, and a 100 megaJule force field surrounded the craft. I punched the door activation button. The outer cargo bay doors banged shut and the environmental system started replacing the atmosphere in the cargo hold. How in the hell did that thing open my cargo bay doors? Why didn't my scanners pick up the ship? A very shapely female exited the little craft. I invited her to my ready room. She said her name was Diamond and explained that her nav system malfunctioned. She needed help to find New Earth. I gave her the coordinates and invited her to stay for dinner. But she was in a hurry.

"Thank you, Steve. I have the coordinates and will leave now for New Earth. You have been very helpful." She headed back to her little ship.

I pressed a button. A totally undetectable tracking device attached itself under her shuttle craft. There was something happening, and I didn't have a clue what it was. The Latium was safely stored in my special safe hidden behind the cargo bay wall.

I watched the monitor. Diamond entered her personal spacecraft and closed the hatch.

"Liberator, this is Diamond requesting permission to disembark."

I opened the cargo bay doors. "Permission granted. Good luck and a smooth voyage." The little ship slipped silently out of the cargo bay into the blackness of space.

The mystery of how the cargo bay doors were opened was solved. I reviewed the security system's recordings. When Diamond appeared in the cargo bay, the system indicated a stowaway was hidden in the cargo-bay control room and initiated the opening of the cargo-bay doors. While I was busy talking to Diamond, the stowaway slipped into the tiny ship from the control room.

I loaded the security system's recordings to find out how her passenger got into my ship. I played the recording. I saw an individual at the airlock hatch. Bang, there was the breach. The scanners showed a figure entering through the airlock, which meant he had the code to the airlock chamber. The entire episode of intruders trying to steal my ship was a fake. Oh crap!

I activated my long-range sensor array. Nothing. I activated the Tracker System. Her ship did show up. A few minutes into the voyage, far to the other side of the solar system, coming from behind the largest planet in the system, was a star ship as large as a moon approaching Diamond at warp 8. That thing was no Alliance ship. The computer could not locate its signature in the database. It had a totally foreign type of design.

I watched the tracker screen as the large ship approached the tiny shuttle craft. Her ship disappeared from the tracker. I looked at the long-range scanner. The giant ship turned and exited the solar system at warp 8. Nothing in the Alliance fleet would be a match. How the hell did they pick up the shuttle at that speed?

Time went by slowly. Subwarp is the pits. I decided to contact Andra on New Earth. I punched up Hypervista frequency NE-67.3 and waited while the alert signal went out. It would take several minutes for the signal to reach New Earth. Finally, a voice came from the com panel.

"This is Andra. Please identify?"

"Andra, this is Steve. Are we secure?"

"Yes."

"I have a request. Scan whatever databases you have access to and identify the signature of the ship I am downloading to you. I'll call you back in a few hours."

I'd never met Andra. April somehow knew of the client and made the deal. Thinking about it, I was uneasy about how this was arranged. I really didn't know anything about them. I remembered April saying their name was Treme'. I looked them up in the Alliance database. The reading was interesting. They were a myth. Humm.

Journal entry - Return to New Earth

April and I were about to enter New Earth's solar system after picking up the Treme` cargo. The ship came out of warp and settled down to docking speed. The autopilot guided the ship flawlessly through the huge doors to its berth below the surface. The landing was perfect. I felt the pods connect to the launch pad. We went through the routine of waiting for the ship to be moved to a berth. A crew removed the cargo and took it away. I closed the cargo bay doors. We got permission to disembark and proceeded to the arrivals hall.

I had not told April about the condo. I wanted it to be a surprise. We took the elevator down 100 levels to my condo. I used the key card to open the door. "You can put your bag in the sleep chamber on the right. I'm in the other chamber."

She looked at me with a quirky smile. I could tell that April was not happy being below the surface. "When will we be able to see the surface and view the seeding project?"

I suspected that she was hoping we could go today. "I don't know. I have to check with Andra. She may not be keen on us leaving the complex without Treme` personnel tagging along. She told me the Alliance insists on a low profile while on the surface. If the sentient species observes any of the AirCars they become very agitated."

"This stinks," April murmured.

I used the condo's com unit and punched up the local number for Andra.

She answered, "Hi, Steve. Welcome back."

"Andra, the cargo has been unloaded. We need to meet. I want to introduce you to my assistant, April.

"Give me your suite number, and I will come as soon as my shift ends. I will be done here in about an hour."

***

The door to my condo buzzed. I opened the door and there stood Andra. She was small-framed with dark hair and couldn't have weighed more than 50 kilograms. Her youthful-looking face smiled and exposed perfect white teeth. She saw April sitting at the table but said nothing.

"Andra, we would like to observe the seeding. When can we go topside?"

"I have to get permission, but maybe later today." She came in and told us all the rules about going to the surface. They were extensive.

Journal entry - The Guardians

Andra left the suite. I pondered if my suspicions were correct about April being part of this. From the way Andra reacted when she heard April's accent, I was beginning to believe the theory. If so, it would answer a lot of questions. I was not sure how to settle the theory in my mind.

When I looked at April, she wore a wide grin. What the hell

does she think is so funny? April got up from the table and went to her bed chamber. She returned with a view pad. She placed it in front of me. She pressed the view button and the screen lit up with an image of the enormous ship I had observed picking up Diamond's personal space craft. I was speechless.

"Does this look familiar?"

I looked at the image. "How...how did you get this?" Wow, this was more than I expected.

"Steve, I have not been completely open with you. Many years ago, I was assigned to recruit you as an unaware vendor for the Treme` group. I am a secret agent in place and on my own. Not even Andra knows who I am."

I sat stunned, to say the least.

April continued. "The New Earth project is one I'm working on at present. We had an agent in place, and she was injured. We had to extract her. I gave out the pass code to your airlock. We put on a show of trying to steal your ship. No, you did not kill our people. They made it appear so. Our agent was successful in getting on board your ship and waited for the pick up by Diamond. All went well, and the agent was picked up. We thought you would never be the wiser. Somehow, you were in the right place at the right time to record the signature of our mother ship, the Vega. I was shocked the Vega's signature had been captured. Our agent had been exposed to a biohazard and had to get to sick bay quickly to be treated. I made a big mistake when I used the Treme` name in telling you about our new client."

I sat there staring at April like an imbecile. "So you are an agent for Treme`, and all those jobs you got for me were somehow part of the Treme` plans." April sat very still.

My com buzzed. It was Andra. "Yes, Andra." I listened as she told me to go to the launch bay in thirty Alliance minutes. "Where are we being taken?" Andra told me not to worry, that we would enjoy the ride. I pressed the disconnect key. "That was Andra and we have to be ready to go for a little ride shortly." I wondered what Andra had in mind.

Journal entry - The Vega

The AirCar was waiting in the launch bay. It had taken us only a few Alliance minutes to arrive at the surface. As soon as we boarded the AirCar and saw Andra at the controls, we relaxed into the passenger seats. Andra pressed the launch sequence key, and the AirCar glided effortless into the deep blue sky.

In a flash, I found myself standing in what appeared to be a large booth. I turned and saw April and Andra were also. A panel opened, and we were ushered to comfortable chairs in a large conference room by a young man.

"Where the blue blazes are we, and how did we get here?" I had an idea, but hearing it would soothe my nerves.

A very young looking-male with a skin-tight, blue uniform sat at the head of the table. He said, "Steve, I'm Mark Young and I'm the mission commander of the Treme`. You are aboard the Starship Vega. You were teleported here from the AirCar which is still in low orbit around the planet. We are about point-five light years away from New Earth's solar system, and you are our guest. All will be explained later. First, I will introduce you to the ship's staff. You already know Andra. To my right is Sarah, and on my left is George. Sarah is the captain of this ship. George is its first officer and security chief." He did not mention April.

So far April had sat very still. She had told me before we left that it had been a long time since she was aboard the Vega, nearly 50 years. Her birth parents died many years ago. On her next birthday, she would turn 78, one year younger than me.

The Oracle

I heard a small humming sound as a portion of the wall parted. A short, portly man appeared at the far end of the table. He had thinning white hair and dark green eyes. The uniform was the same, blue in color and skin-tight, and there were no badges of identification. He sat and folded his hands in front of him on the table.

"My name is Chase. I'm the Oracle of the Guardians. I was elected to this office for 10 years by the Guardian citizens. I'm here to tell you about us and why you were involved in our ventures." The Oracle looked intently into my eyes. "Our mission is to preserve the human race."

The Oracle told the entire story of how Earth had destroyed itself three thousand years before and the three sets of colonists had tried to settle on various planets without a lot of success. He explained the seeding process of planting the original human DNA in an attempt to get the indigenous species to produce peaceful cultures that would end violence and wars. The bad seed was introduced by a warring faction of one of the groups that had split from the Alliance. With my help the bad seed was eliminated, and the bad guys would never know.

***

We were teleported back to the AirCar. Andra piloted us back to the Alliance spaceport. She thanked me and explained that she was being redeployed to the Vega. She hugged April and left. I turned to April, "Well, I'm without a job and have very little money after purchasing the warp manifold and refueling the ship. You have any ideas?"

"We still have the bad guys running around trying to upset the cosmos. Maybe we can help stop them."

***

The *Liberator* attained orbit around New Earth. We retired to my cabin. It had been a long time since April and I had really been together. We slept like the dead. I awoke to find her already awake. She turned to me. "How would you like to become the first contractor to the Guardians employed to stop the bad guys?"

I didn't want to retire anyway. Working with April had lots of benefits.

Poetry

Cat-Napping

BECKY MUSHKO

When I lay me down to sleep,
My cats pile on me in a heap
And snuggle in my face and purr
While I nearly smother in their fur.

Despite this problem, they're just right
To warm me on a winter's night;
But in the summer's balmy air,
I cannot bear their stifling hair.

I sweat profusely with their heat
And try to flip them off my sheet;
But this attempt's in vain because
They cling so tightly with their claws.

No matter how tough I am a fighter,
They only hang on that much tighter.
Every tussle ends in a tie,
And I resolve to let sleeping cats lie.

I've earned a lesson from sleeping with cats
Through all four seasons, and that's
To take the bitter with the sweet
And keep my cool while I take the heat.

A slightly different version of "Cat-Napping" appeared in
Cats, Canines, & Other Critters, Anderie Poetry Press, 1995.

Poetry

One with the Land

BECKY MUSHKO

You'd have been hard-pressed
To separate the old man
From his farm. Bits of red clay
Defied lye soap scrubbing,
Etched deep into the lines
Of his face and hands,
Became part of him.

Most days, God and weather willing,
He'd be out early in one field or another
Plowing, sowing, cultivating, harvesting.
Whatever crop or season demanded,
He'd do. The land worked him hard.
He never begrudged it.

Times he stood back after plowing
To admire his handiwork, he'd let
His eyes caress the perfect furrows
Or the curve of a hill beyond the field,
And something like love or lust
Took root within him.

Under his hand the land would open,
Share its bounty, its secrets,
Sometimes its wrath, demand
His attention like a jealous mistress,
Possess him as much as he possessed it,

Hold him with a grip so sure and firm
There was no other place he desired to be,
No other life he'd dream to live.

Even when death took him,
It didn't take him far—
Only to a corner of the farm
Not much account for growing.
There his land received him
And held him as its own.

Nonfiction

Real Field Trip

BECKY MUSHKO

When I started first grade in 1951, Huff Lane Elementary School in Roanoke, Virginia, was still new. It had been built the previous year to accommodate the kids whose families lived in Dorchester Court, the new housing development across the road from the schoolyard.

On the backside of the schoolyard, where the asphalt playground ended, was the edge of the civilized world—and a huge field where Pete Huff's farm began. Sometimes wheat grew in the field, sometimes corn, and sometimes alfalfa, but the field was always forbidden territory to us kids as we played on the playground. When we climbed to the top of the jungle gym or the metal sliding board, we could catch a glimpse of the dairy barn and the cows in the distance.

One November afternoon, when I was in the third grade, my teacher announced we'd be taking a field trip to that dairy farm. We put on our coats, lined up, and followed our teacher outside. I remember I wore my gray wool coat with a fur collar—a coat I'd inherited from my older cousin Marty and would pass on to my younger cousin Judy. In the early 1950s, hand-me-downs were a fact of life. The coat kept me warm as my classmates and I stepped off the edge of our known world and tromped across the cutover cornfield to the barn.

There we had a close-up view of the Holsteins munching hay while milking machines made strange noises. Someone must have explained the process of getting milk from cow to store, but I don't remember that. What I remember most is the field itself.

Walking across Pete Huff's field ruined me for all future field trips. For years after that third grade excursion, I believed that a field trip should actually involve walking through a field. Consequently, all the other field trips I went on—which involved climbing onto a bus, travelling a few miles, and eventually going into a building—were disappointments.

If the Huff farm was a different world, so were the early 1950s. Back then, our school day began with morning devotions. We stood up, faced the flag, and pledged. The phrase "under God" hadn't been added then, but we didn't need it because we also said the Lord's Prayer. That's how we knew God's name—it was Hallow Ed, as in "Hallow Ed be thy name." And we always sang a song that praised our country. Sometimes we sang "America," and sometimes we sang my favorite, "America the Beautiful."

One morning in late spring, while we sang "America the Beautiful," I looked out the window and actually saw the "spacious skies." They were bright blue. I looked at Pete Huff's field—now planted in wheat—and saw the "amber waves of grain." Beyond the field, I saw the "purple mountains' majesty" of Fort Lewis Mountain and Brushy Mountain in the distance. In front of the mountains, the breeze rippled through the field, which might possibly have been a "fruited plain." That day, God indeed "shed His grace" on me and gave me a glimpse of the America we sang about.

Things have changed since I attended Huff Lane School. In the 1970s, I-581 bisected Pete Huff's farm. In the 1980s, what was left of the farm became Valley View Shopping Center. For a while, the school became "Huff Lane Microvillage"; then it became Huff Lane Intermediate School. By the 1990s, the asphalt playground had been replaced by grass. The jungle gym and sliding board were gone. A high gray wall with mountains painted on it separated what was left of the playground from what was no longer farm.

Then, a few years ago, the school closed and was razed to build a motel.

In Huff Lane's final years, its students probably never sang "America the Beautiful" or any other song. They no doubt still said the pledge, but the Lord's Prayer had been replaced by a moment of silence. Likely, they never knew Hallow Ed.

Whenever I drive through Valley View Mall, where Pete Huff's farm used to be, I pass close to where my former school once was, and I feel a little sorry for all the students who'll never get to see the world the way I once did—and who can never step off the edge of a playground and take a real field trip.

Nonfiction

Romancing the Story

BECKY MUSHKO

Nearly two decades ago, I spent a few weeks reading romances. I'm not a big romance fan, but I'd heard romances are easier to sell than most genres. Indeed, even Harlequin, a major romance publisher, posted on its website guidelines for its multitude of imprints. Consequently, I decided to investigate the genre.

I read four romances—a Harlequin Super-Romance written by an online acquaintance, a Harlequin Intrigue Gothic Romance whose cover caught my eye at Wal-Mart, and two print-on-demand ones written by acquaintances. I also skimmed through *Writing a Romance Novel for Dummies* and looked at a bunch of on-line suggestions. From my reading and research, I concluded the following:

1. The heroine will be young and beautiful. She will not have a common name, such as Mary or Anne. Her name will be either at least three syllables or exotic. Katherine is an acceptable name, as is Virginia or Elizabeth. She will be intelligent and might even hold a high-paying job, but she will have lapses of common sense— especially where a handsome man is concerned—and, despite being in her late twenties or early thirties, she will be a virgin or at least won't have had meaningful sex or maybe won't have had any sex for a very long time. Or possibly a combination of those. Anyhow, she will either be innocent or appear to be innocent. She will have long hair and legs, but not hairy legs. While she will have good fashion sense, she will not necessarily wear sensible shoes. Odds are good that she might have a secret about her past.

2. The hero, who must appear within the first five pages, will have a one syllable, masculine name—Flint, Brett, or Chad, but not Bob or Fred. He might have a two-syllable name if it sounds old-fashioned and respectable. Harry or Robert is an acceptable name,

but not Horace or Herbert. His muscles will be taut. It doesn't matter which muscles—perhaps his chest, his arms, or buttocks—the latter revealed by his well-fitting riding pants as he gallops his stallion. (Note: If horses are involved, the hero will ride a stallion. The heroine, of course, will ride a mare.) Not only will his muscles be taut, the appropriate ones will ripple. The hero will also have good hair and lots of it on both head and chest. The head hair will be wavy. If his eyes are blue, they won't be *just* blue—they'll be ice blue or steel blue. Odds are good that he'll also have a secret about his past.

3. There will most likely be a young female character, probably the daughter/niece/ward of the hero. The heroine will serve as her role-model—or at least will be able to reach her in a way that no one else has been able to, because the young female character has issues of some kind. Possibly several kinds. While this character might make some bad choices or cause the death of a minor character, she will nonetheless be good at heart.

4. Several other characters will be mysterious and appear bad to throw the reader off track until it is revealed that they are really good at heart—or at least misunderstood and just not very attractive.

5. There must be an evil character, who possibly works for the hero, is related to the hero, was once married to the hero, or once lusted for the former wife of the hero. He or she will either lust for one of the main characters or will try to bankrupt them if a heavily mortgaged estate is involved. This evil character will not be successful in his or her evil designs and will probably be killed by falling off a cliff or something shrouded in fog.

6. Other important stuff: Fog is an essential element in a romance, but the fog will lift so that the main characters can see something revealing. Often the action takes place on a large estate (that may or may not have fallen into decline) or an exotic vacation spot. If any animals are featured, they will be horses, which someone else will groom and have ready. Naturally both hero and heroine will be excellent riders. Cats and dogs, for some reason, are not conducive to romances and don't play major parts. Small

rodents—ferrets, gerbils, or hamsters—are also not the stuff romances are made of.

7. Bodily functions in romances usually involve the heart. Hearts tilt, flip, race, thump, thud, clutch, or are touched in some way—but usually not physically. Stomachs tighten, churn, or clench. Breathing is important; breath is held, taken away, or gasped. No one has bad breath—or bad hair—unless it's the evil character or possibly the misunderstood minor characters. The main characters do not actually sweat, no matter how passionate the moment, but they might glisten.

8. As for passion, sex between the hero and heroine is usually done standing up and possibly in the shower or under a waterfall or perhaps in a horse's stall. It won't happen until late in the book, and it will come (no pun intended) as a surprise to both characters who won't have any trouble shucking their clothes. The word "shuck" will not, or course, be mentioned, nor any word that rhymes with it. Either the hero will use a condom (which he will have handy even though he had no previous intention of having sex) or else the heroine might have had a hysterectomy. After their wild and passionate tryst, during which they do not sweat, the hero and heroine will realize they should be married and will make plans to do so as soon as a few pesky plot twists are untwisted—such as trying to figure how to get back into the right century or figure who is trying to kill them. Or both.

9. There will be lots of plot twists with seemingly loose ends. For instance, one character might be revealed to be a long-lost someone or other who is important to another character. However, by the end of the book, all the loose ends are untwisted and tied up, the evil person meets with a very bad end, the family fortune is restored or a main character gets a good job, and all the nice people live happily ever after, even if it means the heroine has to give up her great job to marry the hero. Good triumphs over evil, vice triumphs over virtue, yada-yada-yada.

From reading romances and articles about how to write them, I was prompted to attempt a synopsis of the romance novel that I will never write. Here it is:

Thudding Hearts and Galloping Passions

Twenty-year-old Celestine, having left the Sacred Heart and Inner Sanctum Convent where she had spent her entire life in quiet contemplation and computer studies, finds herself in Virginia horse country near the University of Virginia where she had allegedly come to study for an advanced degree in computer systems administration and cyber-philosophy after convincing the head nun, Sister Mary Ignatius, that the convent's website needed someone with more training, especially in the interactive areas of the on-line confessional and virtual rosary.

Celestine is in somewhat of a mental fog, having recently learned that she is the illegitimate daughter of Sister Mary Magdalene and Father Vinnie, who'd had a brief but passionate tryst in one of the confessionals shortly after Mass, where Father Vinnie's rippling muscles had excited the repressed emotions of most of the nuns, except for Sister Mary Butch and her very good friend, the hot-blooded Scottish nun, Sister Mary Bruce, both of whom just happened to notice unusually passionate sounds emanating from one of the confessionals that also appeared to be rocking. Thinking they'd witnessed a miracle and hoping to score points with Mother Superior, they immediately reported what they'd witnessed. Mother Superior, upon opening the confessional, found the disheveled nun and the defrocked priest in what was not a missionary position. Vowing to keep their sin secret so as to not stain the otherwise immaculate reputation of the Sacred Heart and Inner Sanctum Convent, she sequestered away Sister Mary Magdalene and gave Father Vinnie a missionary position in Bolivia. Nine months later, Celestine was born, and Mother Superior pretended that she'd found the baby on a doorstep, which wasn't so much a lie as it was a sin of omission about the doorstep actually being the one to Sister Mary Magdalene's garret. Sister Mary Magdalene, under a vow of silence, kept her mouth shut.

Celestine prospers in the care of the nuns, although they are unable to give her a sense of fashion, a knowledge of pop culture, or any hair or make-up tips. They do, however, allow her full access to the convent's computer system, where she finds out these things for herself while she grows into a beautiful woman with long flaxen hair, an impish smile, and a set of 38-Ds that a nun's habit would never be able to conceal, should she decide to become one, but that career choice holds no appeal for her.

Having arrived at UVA too late to gain entrance to a very competitive program, Celestine is at a loss as to what to do—both at the moment and with her life. While sipping latte in a cyber-cafe, she answers an online ad for a governess at a nearby estate.

Having walked the entire six miles in her Pradas and having bumped into several large trees in the fog, she arrives late and somewhat worse for wear. Seeing the lights on in the stable, she wanders in where Ambrose the stable-boy mistakes her for a woman of easy virtue and is about to force his unwanted attentions on her in Lord Dunsinane's stall, when Harold Fairchilde rides into the barn on his stallion and rescues her. Tossing Lord Dunsinane's reins to Ambrose, Harold removes his riding jacket to real massive rippling muscles and wraps the coat about the shivering Celestine, whose heart thumps and whose breath is momentarily taken away when she looks into his icy steel blue eyes and sees what a hunk he is.

Harold carries Celestine up the curved and cobblestoned drive to Monte Hall, an imposing Georgian structure that the moonlight reveals is a bit worse for wear, a detail that only adds to its charm and mystery. Ensconcing her on a burgundy leather club chair in the library, he pokes the fire to warm her spirits, but her heart is warmed at the sight of his taut buttocks as he bends to tend the fire before offering her a glass of sherry.

While she sips sherry and basks in the decadent splendor of the library, Harold tells her to call him Hal ("Despite the pretentiousness of the place, we're pretty informal around here," he says) and informs her about his ward, 12-year-old Penelope, and how he's been unable to reach her since she arrived two months earlier following the untimely deaths of her parents who ventured too close to an active volcano while doing a photo shoot at some exotic location (Note to self: look up exotic locales that have active volcanoes). Penelope survived only because she disobeyed her parents and didn't follow them to the volcano's edge. (Note: Do volcanoes have edges?) While Hal tells her that he didn't actually know Penelope's parents (Penelope's father Vincent Vermicelli was a friend of Hal's maternal grandfather Guido), he is flattered that they entrusted him with her care and he was looking for something meaningful in life since he has so much money left to him by Guido that he doesn't have to actually work.

Hal is, however, concerned that Penelope spends all her waking hours on the Internet instead of riding to the hounds, listening to loud music, studying modern dance, writing angst-filled poetry, defying authority, or becoming infatuated with the stable-boys as any normal incredibly wealthy 12-year-old would do instead of sharing her feelings with him. The expression "sharing feelings" touches Celestine's heart, so she tells Hal she will take the job. He orders the old housekeeper, Mrs. Bartleby, to show her to her room. Mrs. Bartleby says she would prefer not to, a phrase that she often repeats during the next several months while Celestine works as governess, but she shows Celestine to the third-floor room anyhow.

To make an incredibly long story short, Celestine hacks into Penelope's computer and discovers that Penelope is actually eighteen and was planted by her family, the Vincent Vermicelli branch of the Blue Ridge Mafia, to find where their old rival Guido Garibaldi hid the jewels he converted his drug money into after buying the estate. However, Celestine is infatuated with Hal and forgets to tell him what she discovered until they are out riding one fateful foggy morning. Celestine, although not raised around horses, is nevertheless a natural horsewoman and is soon jumping four-foot-high fences and galloping over the incredibly picturesque and rugged countryside on her mare Birnum Wood.

On this fateful morning, Ambrose the stable-boy, jealous of the attention Celestine is giving Hal and vice-versa, neglects to tell her that Birnum Wood is in heat. As Hal and Celestine race their horses toward the (insert name of Nelson County River here— preferably one with very high banks), Hal reins back Lord Dunsinane, the better to admire Celestine's up-tuned bottom revealed by her designer riding breeches as she gets in perfect two-point position to jump an imposing downed tree. Lord Dunsinane, sniffing the air and realizing that Birnum Wood is in heat, whinnies to the mare who turns in mid-air and comes to Dunsinane who mounts her.

Celestine tumbles off and rolls clear of the coupling horses, although she is left breathless. Hal dismounts and, realizing that Celestine is the woman of his dreams, scoops her up and carries her to the fallen tree, where she regains her breath as the fog clears to reveal Dunsinane in all his stallion manhood doing what stallions do to mares in heat.

This gives Hal and Celestine an idea, and fortunately they are able to lean against the tree whilst expending their pent-up passions upon each other while a light rain begins to fall. Fortunately, Hal discovers a condom in his pocket. Hal then proposes to Celestine, who tells him she will think about it and then reveals what she knows about Penelope. Their conversation is interrupted by a loud splash, as if a body fell off the very high bank and into the river, but the rain has stopped and fog has returned so they can't see who it is.

They ride back to Monte Hall, stopping as soon as they see it to admire the full Monte for a breath-clenching moment, and then racing full gallop to find Mrs. Bartleby bound and gagged, Hal's desk broken open, a large hole in the library wall, and one of the BMWs and a large roll of duct tape missing. Of course Penelope is gone, too, as is Ambrose.

Fortunately, Celestine remembers accessing a travel site on Penelope's computer, so she is able to provide full details to the police, who arrest Penelope for speeding on I-64, recover the jewels that she took from inside the wall, and find the duct-taped body of Ambrose (who is—or more correctly was—actually Penelope's lover as well a spy for the Blue Ridge Mafia) bobbing about in the river.

Penelope, repentant for all the trouble she caused, begs forgiveness from everyone and makes a full confession. They finally remember to unsaddle the horses and ungag Mrs. Bartleby, not that it makes any difference because she would prefer not to comment. Soon the FBI arrests Vincent Vermicelli, who did not die in the volcano, and discovers that he once hid out in the Sacred Heart and Inner Sanctum Convent twenty-three years earlier by assuming the guise of a priest. . . .

That's as far as I got before deciding I will stick to writing Appalachian fiction or blog-posts about my cats, both of which are considerably easier to write than romance, so I will leave it to you, Gentle Reader, to figure out the ending. If you might be interested in writing romance novels yourself, I have a barely-used copy of *Writing a Romance Novel for Dummies* (copyright 2004) that I could be persuaded to part with. For the right price, of course.

This essay was based on a 2006 post, "Romancing the Story," on Becky Mushko's *Peevish Pen* blog.

Fiction

Making Changes

BECKY MUSHKO

When Trina ran off to Richmond to "find herself" by becoming a cocktail waitress, I made some serious changes in my life. One thing, I lost my job at her daddy's driveway paving company.

"Sonny, the job came with the marriage," was how he put it. "The marriage ends, so does the job."

Another thing, our doublewide was on his land. The same conditions applied.

"My little gal musta had a good reason," her daddy said when I tried to reason with him. "You musta done something. Now I'll give you two weeks to git your sorry self out."

I tried to tell him I hadn't done nothing. I worked hard for him all day, and after I had a few beers with my buddies I went straight home to Trina. Then she'd light into me.

"Do this, do that! Mow the yard. Take me out to eat. We never go anywhere. You don't pay me enough attention!" was how she'd go on.

I tried to make her understand that after a hard day's work, a man just wants to come home and lay on the couch and watch TV and have his supper brought to him and maybe git a little loving later on after he's rested up. It wasn't like she had to work or nothing. All she had to do was clean up the doublewide, iron my shirts, have my meals cooked, and watch TV.

Her watching TV—now that was the problem! She watched all them talk shows, and they give her ideas about "finding herself" and "being fulfilled" and crap. Her sister Ruby Jo in Richmond who had a batch of ex-husbands didn't help none—writing and telling Trina about her big job and all the money she made in tips, telling about all the things to do in Richmond, and how Trina could come live with her if she wanted to. I know for a fact what was in them letters. I snuck and read them.

To top it off, she didn't even have the nerve to tell me to my face that she was leaving. Just left me a note and hopped on the Greyhound bus like she was Queen of England or something.

"I need some space," her note said, "and I just can't communicate with you."

Now that is an out-and-out lie. Anything she ever wanted to say to me, she did. She never was one to mince words, neither. Sometimes it was all I could do to put up with her nagging.

"I need to find myself," her note went on, "and I can't find fulfillment with you in a two-bit trailer in Floyd County."

Anyhow, wasn't nothing to do but pack up my clothes and leave. Since her daddy had co-signed the trailer loan, let him make the payments. At least my truck was mine, so I took off in it. Didn't take me no time to find a job driving heavy equipment to build what they call the "smart road" in Montgomery County. I got myself a room in a old house west of Salem, which put me halfway between work and the big city of Roanoke. If Trina could go off to a big city—well, so could I. There was a bunch of fast food restaurants nearby, and that took care of getting something to eat.

Things looked pretty good for a while. All day I'd run a front-end loader, then I'd stop by Hardee's or McDonald's for supper, make a run to Quikette for a six-pack, and drink beer and watch some TV until I went to sleep. Wasn't long till I ran out of clean clothes, so I went over to Wal-Mart which was right across the highway from where I lived and got me some more t-shirts, jeans, and BVDs. A week later I was back in the same fix. I decided I'd better break down and do some washing, so I stuffed all my clothes in a couple of pillowcases, stopped by a phone booth to look in the phone book, and found me the address of a nearby laundromat.

I was pushing everything I owned but the clothes on my back into a big washing machine so I could get away with just doing one load, when a voice behind me said, "You're new at this, aren't you?"

I turned around, and there stood the best-looking girl I'd ever seen close up in real life. She looked good enough to turn letters on a TV game show, she was that good-looking! She had long, dark hair and wore one of them tight little V-neck shirts that showed off her assets real good. It took me a minute to get my voice back, and then I said, "Yeah."

"Let me show you, then," she said, and pulled all my clothes out of the washer. "You got to separate your whites and colors. If you put those red t-shirts in with your briefs, you'll be wearing pink underpants. I might be wrong, but you don't look like the pink underpants type."

"I'm not," I said. Her talking about my underwear like that made me think she might be trying to pick me up, which was all right by me. "I don't know nothing about doing wash. My wife always done it till she run off." Then I told her about Trina and how bad she done me.

"You poor baby," the girl said. "I can't imagine any woman leaving a hunk like you."

Now I was pretty sure she was trying to pick me up. I couldn't believe my luck—a good-looking girl who did laundry.

After she separated the clothes into piles—and it was a thrill, I'll tell you, when her hands touched my BVDs—she said, "Where's your detergent?"

"Huh?" I said.

"Your detergent. Soap. What you wash with?"

"Oh, I don't reckon I got any. I just figured the water'd be enough," I said.

"You've got a lot to learn, Sonny," she said, "if you want to make it on your own."

"How'd you know my name?" I asked. "How'd you know my name is Sonny?"

"Lucky guess," she said, and smiled a smile just full of white even teeth set off by bright red lipstick on her lips.

"Well, what's your name?" I asked. "You know mine, but I

don't know yours."

"Dana," she said. "I'm Dana."

Then she stuck out her hand for me to shake. It was a soft hand with long, thin fingers with long nails painted the same color red as her lips. You could tell right off that her hand wasn't a hand that did heavy work.

"I'll let you borrow some of mine," she said, "seeing that you're not used to domestic work."

She explained how much detergent I had to use and showed me how to measure it out and put it in the washer. She poured some bleach into my load of underwear.

"It makes things whiter," she explained. "Now you remember all this, Sonny. Next time you do laundry, there might not be anybody around to help you."

I bought us coffee out of the coffee machine by the door, and we set there drinking our coffee and watching my clothes flop around in the washer just like we was watching TV. We talked some more, and I told her about my job, and she told me about how she was originally from Pulaski and how she worked at the Salem Winn-Dixie and that she sometimes took classes at Virginia Western Community College. She lived in an apartment in Roanoke right near the college, but she always did her laundry on her way home from work on account it was easier.

Whooee, I thought to myself, without even trying I met a good-looking girl who does laundry and has her own apartment and is smart besides. This was the kind of girl I'd like to see more of, but I didn't want to rush things and have her think bad of me.

When her clothes came out of the drier, I watched her fold them. Dana had lots of different-colored lacy underwear things— some of it real flimsy-looking. It was the kind of stuff I used to want Trina to wear, but she wouldn't because she said stuff like that itched like crazy with all that lace and stuff. I noticed that none of Dana's bras were padded like Trina's had been. I sneaked a look at a bra label. It said 36C. Dana caught me looking and I musta turned red.

"Well," she said, "I got to be going. I've got an early class tomorrow. It was real nice to meet you, Sonny."

Then she was gone. I hadn't even asked for her phone number or nothing. When my clothes were dry, I didn't bother with folding them like I would've if Dana had still been there—just stuffed them in my pillowcases. I made up my mind then to run by Wal-Mart next chance I got and buy myself some of those low-slung colored briefs so the next woman who handled them would be impressed by my style.

I thought about Dana on and off during the next week. I might've drove by the laundromat a time or two, but didn't see her there. Next time I did laundry, only an old man who looked kind of homeless was there. Every evening after I got off work, I took to driving up Colonial Avenue that ran past the community college, but I never saw Dana there. Finally, I decided I probably could use a few groceries, so I looked up the address of Winn-Dixie and stopped by there one evening. Sure enough, there she was working the express checkout line. I made sure I didn't buy too much so it'd look like a coincidence I had to use her line.

At first I don't think she knew me. At least she didn't look up. She was just totaling up my bag of chips and six-pack and Doritos and two-liter bottle of Coke as quick as all get out.

"You want to go out and do some laundry after you get off tonight?" I said. I thought that sounded real cool.

She looked at me. "Oh, Sonny?" she said.

"That's me," I said.

"It looks like you eat about like you do laundry," she said as she bagged my groceries. "This won't make much of a meal."

"You know what we call a seven-course meal where I come from?" I asked her.

She shook her head.

"A possum and a six pack," I said.

Then she smiled that real nice smile at me and handed me my bag. An old lady behind me cleared her throat like she wanted me to hurry up.

"Do you want to, uh, go out sometime?" I said. "Not necessarily to do laundry. Maybe grab a cup of coffee or something?"

"Well, sure," she said, just like that, and then she wrote her number on the bag. "Give me a call in a day or two."

I was flat out walking on air when I left the Winn-Dixie. I called her the next day and we went bowling. Dana was a real good bowler for a girl. In fact, she beat me all three games. I was hoping she'd ask me to come in when I took her home, but she said she had to study. I guess she could see I looked disappointed.

"Tell you what, Sonny," she said. "Why don't I show you how to cook? You come on over about six-thirty this Friday night."

"You want me to bring anything?" I said

"Not possum," she said. "And no six pack either. Just bring yourself and an appetite."

That was easy enough to do. I got there about ten minutes early. When I knocked, Dana hollered for me to let myself in. She was still in the shower and she'd be out in a few minutes, she said, so I was to make myself at home.

She had a real nice apartment. You could tell it had a woman's touch, everything was just as neat and picked up. I looked at some of the books on her shelf and noticed a Pulaski County High School yearbook. It must be hers, I thought to myself, so I thumbed through it to see what she looked like in high school. The name "Dan" was in the front of it, and when I tried to find her, all I found was Dan who looked just like her. Doggone if she don't have a twin brother, I decided. About that time she came out wearing a real low-cut outfit that looked like she was dressed for some action later.

"Your secret is out," I said. "I found your yearbook."

"Oh?" she said. She looked kinda surprised. "What secret?"

"About you being a twin," I said. "This Dan is your twin brother, ain't he?"

"You might say that," she said. She was playing real coy.

"But I can't find you in here," I said. "Were you absent the day they took pictures?"

"Yeah, I wasn't there much in high school," she said.

"Where's Dan now?" I said. "He live around here, or is he still in Pulaski?"

"We've lost touch," she said. "He's not around much anymore."

"That's a shame," I said, "y'all being twins and all. I don't see my sister much either. We used to fight like cats and dogs."

"Yeah," she said, "I know the feeling. You got an appetite?"

I had to admit I did. In fact there were several appetites I had, if you get my drift. She led me into this little kitchenette where she had several pots on the stove.

"You stir this," she said, "while I toss the salad."

She gave me a big wooden spoon and I stirred. The kitchenette was so small, we kept bumping into each other, which didn't bother me one bit. I musta been stirring too fast on account she put her hand over top of mine and showed me how to stir slower and in a better way so the stuff in the pot got mixed together better. I was getting to like this cooking stuff.

When we ate, everything tasted a whole lot better than Hardee's, but maybe it was just because it was something different. We had spaghetti, and what I'd been stirring had been the sauce—only it wasn't Chef Boyardee like Trina used to make, it was put together special from scratch.

This Dana is something else, I thought. This is the kind of girl I ought to of married in the first place. She was a real woman—not the kind who'd have to run off and "find herself" neither. I was glad I'd found her.

After we finished eating, we did the dishes in that little-bitty kitchenette. She washed and I dried, and we kept bumping into each other again. Our hands touched every time she handed me a dish. It was the first time I ever did dishes, and I got to admit it wasn't half bad.

After that, we sat on her couch and watched some TV and drank coffee. Then she poured us some white wine, which I always thought was kind of a sissy drink, but I decided what the heck, everything else has worked out, so I tried it. At first it took some getting used to, but by the third glass, it wasn't half-bad either. Dana explained not to chug it, but to sip it, and that helped. Wasn't long till that wine made me feel real friendly, and Dana didn't mind a bit that I started kissing on her. She even started kissing me back, and that's when I suggested that we maybe go into the other room. She said she didn't think that was a very good idea, and maybe it was time for me to go.

"Things are happening too fast," she said, "and you're still married."

That was so. I guess I should've been glad to find an old-fashioned girl like Dana, but I was some disappointed, too. I told her I'd call her next day, and she said that would be all right.

Sure enough, I called her and she didn't say a word about asking me to leave the night before. I asked her out again and she said yes. We started dating on pretty much a regular basis. It was driving me crazy that she'd wear all these sexy outfits and wouldn't let me do nothing. When I said something about it, Dana said I'd just have to be patient with her. Meanwhile, she started doing a few things to kind of distract me—if you know what I mean—things I'd once suggested to Trina that she try, but Trina had told me won't no way she'd do stuff like that. By then, my divorce was in the works. I made up my mind that when it was final, I'd pop the question to Dana. A man don't find a girl like her everyday.

One time when I was using Dana's bathroom, I happened to open her medicine cabinet. There was a whole bunch of medicine bottles in there. None of the prescriptions sounded familiar, but they all had her name on them. I wondered if she might not have some kind of bad disease that she didn't want to tell me about, and maybe that was why she kept putting me off and why she never let me see her naked. I felt like we knew each other good enough for her to confide in me, though.

"Dana," I said when I came out, "are all them medicines yours? Are you sick and not telling me?"

"They're mine," she said, and didn't even fuss at me for snooping. "I'm not exactly sick. I just have this condition that requires medication."

"Oh," I said. "It ain't something I can catch, is it?"

"No, nothing like that," she said. "It's sort of a female problem."

"Is that why you won't—well, you know?" I didn't know how

to say it in a nice way. She was too much of a lady for me to say what I was really thinking.

"Yes," she said, "that's why."

Well, that explained things. Likely she couldn't do *it* without hurting herself. I hoped it wasn't cancer or something.

"Will you ever be able—?"

"Yes," she said, "but I have to have a little corrective surgery. There's been an insurance problem, so I can't have the surgery done right away."

"You poor baby," I said, and held her close to me. "Don't you worry none. I'll be here for you."

I decided Dana was a girl definitely worth waiting for. By then, it was only a few days until my divorce was final, and I figured I wouldn't have to wait very long. I'd saved up a few dollars so I went shopping for a ring.

The night I'd signed the papers and was finally free of Trina, Dana had cooked a special supper to celebrate. Afterwards, we sat on the couch and drank some kind of fancy coffee with whipped cream on top. About halfway through my cup, I reached in my pocket and pulled out the ring. Dana looked like she didn't know what to say.

"Well, is it yes?" I asked.

"Wait right here," she said and went into the bathroom.

I'd taken a big gulp of that coffee about the time she came out wearing only a towel around her waist. Oh wow, I thought, tonight's the night! Life can't get much better than this.

"Sonny, before I answer your question, there's something you need to know," she said. "You might even want to take back your offer."

I couldn't take my eyes off her 36C's. The only thing that would be better than them was if she'd drop her towel.

Then she dropped her towel.

I couldn't believe what I was looking at. I thought my eyes would fall out. I choked on my coffee. It was almost more than I could stand!

"Dana!" I said when I got my voice back. "Why didn't you tell me you're a guy?"

"I should have," she said, "but I kept hoping the insurance would approve the rest of the surgery and then you'd never know. They paid for the breast implants and the hormone therapy, so I naturally thought—well, I won't blame you, Sonny, if you walk out that door and never come back."

"Does Dan know?" I wondered out loud.

"There is no Dan," she said. "Well, not exactly. Dan and Dana are parts of the same person. But if Dana comes out, then Dan has to go. Dana had to hide for a long time, and she doesn't want to stay hidden anymore. Does this make sense to you?"

I shook my head. This was way too much for me to think about. One minute I'm the happiest man on earth, and the next—well, this kinda change wasn't something a man would expect to happen when he pops the question to the girl of his dreams.

"You lied to me," I said. You said you had a female problem—"

"I didn't lie," Dana said. "My problem is that I'm female emotionally and I want to be female physically. If they hadn't changed the insurance requirements, I would be a complete female by now. As it is, I have to save up so University of Virginia Hospital will do the surgery. Then you won't even know that I was ever a guy."

"I won't?" I said. "You mean, there wouldn't be any way of telling—?"

"No," Dana said.

"This is something I gotta think about," I told her. Him. Whoever. "I just can't deal with all that's happened tonight. I gotta go."

When I went out the door, she—he—started to cry. I was so upset I forgot to take the ring with me. I went straight to the nearest bar and got as drunk as I could. Even then, I still couldn't forget.

Well, it goes without saying that I didn't sleep much that night. I couldn't help thinking about the girl I loved and how she was really a guy. It was like something you'd see on Jerry Springer or Maury, only this was my real life.

The next morning I called in sick. I laid around all morning thinking until I made up my mind what I had to do. I stopped for coffee to go and then drove over to Winn-Dixie and went to Dana's checkout line. I could see her eyes looked red. She must've cried a lot after I left.

"Dana, we got to talk," I said.

"I get a break in ten minutes," she said. "You go wait in the truck, and I'll come out then."

I did what she said. I sat there drinking my coffee and waiting and trying to figure out the right words to say. Wasn't long till she come out and slipped in the seat next to me. She twisted the ring off her finger.

"I suppose you want this back," Dana said, as she put it in my hand.

"Dana," I said. "I been thinking. I got a few thousand dollars coming to me from the divorce settlement—half of what Trina's Daddy sold the doublewide for. I saved up a few thousand more since I been working. If that ain't enough for your operation, maybe I get a bank loan or sell the truck or something."

I slipped the ring back on her finger.

"You mean you still want to marry me?" she said.

"I guess so," I said, "but it's gonna take some getting used to that you was once a guy. You gotta be patient with me."

Then she smiled a big smile and kissed me smack on the lips right there in the parking lot. I hoped anybody who seen us didn't know her secret. I wouldn't want it spread around that I was the type who made a habit of kissing guys in Winn-Dixie parking lots in broad daylight.

Well, I thought to myself, being married to somebody like Dana is gonna be a big change for me in more ways than one. Good thing I'm used to making changes.

"Making Changes" originally appeared in *Virginia Adversaria*, Spring 2001, and the Amazon Kindle e-book *Over Coffee*.

Fiction

The Damsel and the Frog: A Fairy Tale

BECKY MUSHKO

Once upon a time, a damsel galloping her milk-white steed across the kingdom chanced upon a pond. She reined in her steed that he might drink while she admired her reflection in the clear water. The steed's lips had no sooner touched water and the damsel had no sooner gazed upon her reflection whereupon a frog leapt from the depths.

"Oh, fair damsel!" exclaimed the frog, perching upon a stone and peering at her with rather bugged-out eyes. "I have been wishing and waiting for you! You see, a witch has cast a spell upon me, and a kiss from you will return me to my human self."

"What's in it for me?" the damsel asked. She normally wouldn't speak to strangers, but a talking frog rather intrigued her.

"I am a prince," the frog replied, "under the spell until a fair young maiden like yourself bestows a kiss upon my lips." He expected her to alight from her steed and rush toward him, but the damsel did not. Thinking she needed a bit of encouragement or she was too dense to get what he was saying, the frog prompted, "Kiss me, and you shall be my princess."

"Uh, exactly what does being a princess entail?" the damsel asked. She had been warned by her fairy godmother to thoroughly check out her prospects and possibly get a pre-nup that was favorable to her. She dismounted to get a closer look at the frog.

"Why, you shall sit by my side, and we will reign over the kingdom together," the frog said. Though, truth be told, he wondered why he had to explain this. "At least after my father, the king, dies."

"And what shall we do before he, uh, croaks?" the damsel

asked.

Ignoring the damsel's rather tasteless pun, the frog replied, "Why, we shall wear fine clothes and dine upon fine food and host balls and have servants wait upon us. Plus we will spend a goodly part of our days sitting upon our thrones and listening to entreaties from the common folk."

"That sounds dreadfully boring," the damsel said. "Will I still be able to gallop my steed across the countryside whenever the mood strikes me? Meet my friends for a draught of ale at Ye Olde Publick House? Frolic across the meadow or dance around the May-pole?"

"I'm afraid not," the frog said. "Security regulations prohibit reckless riding, frolicking with the commoners, ale-quaffing in public, May-pole dancing, and all that sort of thing. It doesn't set a good example."

A fly flitted past, and the frog snapped it with his tongue and gobbled it down. The princess shuddered.

"Well," she said, remembering that the only prince she'd glimpsed at the last ball was rather short and not at all handsome, "being a princess doesn't sound like much fun."

"You'll get used to it. Now are you going to kiss me or not?" The frog puckered as much as an amphibian could pucker.

"I think not," the damsel replied. Having noticed a bit of fly-wing on the frog's lower lip, she realized she'd never find happiness with a husband who ate flies. "I do not wish to live such a restrained life. But I do wish you success in escaping your frog-bound existence."

She then mounted her milk-white steed and galloped away toward Ye Olde Publick House where she'd tell her friends about the talking frog and perhaps indulge in a bit of pole-dancing after she'd quaffed a few draughts of ale.

"Ingrate!" the frog yelled. "I so terribly wish the next female who comes to this pond realizes what a catch I am."

No sooner had he voiced his wish than a female great blue heron alighted in the pond, spied the frog, and gobbled him up. She'd been wishing for a tasty snack and couldn't believe her good luck.

Hence, the damsel, the frog, and the heron all got their wishes. But only two lived happily ever after.

—The End—

Nonfiction

Living Green

SUE PATTERSON

Recycling is very important to keep our Good Earth livable for the next generations. Reuse, reduce, recycle! I'm also into organic gardening and composting.

I have even recycled my first husband, making him my third and forever husband. We won't talk about the in-between husband. All three of my children are also all of the three children of my recycled husband.

Our house was purchased by me when I was an independent woman. No husband in the picture!

It became "our" house on March 22, 2003. Chuck is a very handy man around the house. The first thing he did was to make me a little studio and a storage shed out of a barely-under-roof lean-to building out back in the woods. Then he converted the garage on the lower level of the house into his man cave.

Next he turned the carport into the dining room. That really increased our floor space.

When he finished expanding the deck from behind the kitchen all the way to the pool and pool house, we agreed that he should be rewarded by purchasing a very manly gas grill, complete with a VT logo on the vinyl cover.

Then he decided to make a sunroom of the original deck behind the kitchen! It is a wonderful space. Due to a few missteps, we waited several years to finally decorate it. Twelve skylights that leaked when it rained had to be re-installed before we dared to have carpet put down.

The carpet is installed, and the staining and painting will be done this week.

The process of the carpet delivery and installation was very bad for my health. I call it A Tale of Two Tables, a Big Roll of Carpet, and Chuck!

We had to remove everything from the sunroom before the carpet could be installed. The big roll was in the dining room beside the dinner table. Chuck and I were carrying the coffee table to the other end of the dining room.

I should NOT have been backing up with my end of the coffee table, but I was, and Chuck was on the other end. I stumbled a little and, instead of holding steady or pulling back, Chuck pushed forward and sent me flying over the big roll of carpet. My chin got pinched between the Two Tables. List of injuries: my tongue was bitten bloody, my right knee was scraped, and the right side of my head was bumped.

Thankfully, my jaw was not broken, but when I went to my dentist for a previously-scheduled crown prep two days later, she decided to put it off until my tongue and trauma were better.

***

How can you remember where anything is unless you have a place for it? Having my things in plain sight is key to my organizational skills. I really don't like 'junk' drawers.

The drawers containing various utensils and supplies in our kitchen are orderly but in need of a sorting out…the meat tenderizer hammer has never been used, and the rolling pin hasn't been used in years. So far, the kitchen-sorting is all still in my mind. I will physically get to it one of these days.

I have been working on the drawers in my bedroom. A few weeks ago, I discovered a drawer full of sweaters. We are still in winter, and none of them had been worn since last winter! There they are all, carefully aligned in three stacks, just waiting to be worn.

All of the drawers holding my clothing are kept in good order. Usually there is no need to straighten the contents. Laundry is folded and carefully put away. There is a drawer full of belts. I never wear them anymore. My waistline is not so defined as it once was. Not that I am complaining. Praise the Lord that I can still do most activities that need doing.

However, when I came to my drawer of 'unmentionables', undies, "smalls" (a neighbor that we shared a clothesline with in Auckland, New Zealand, requested a certain day of the week to hang her "smalls"), or panties, I realized that there was a layer of thong underwear! Honestly, I only tried one pair on back in the day that Darling Daughter convinced me that panty lines showing through tights are very uncool. I think she even bought them for me.

Disposing of barely worn thongs can be a problem. I am a recycler and hate to throw away anything that still has usefulness. Remembering all of the keeping-them-sanitary measures that we had to take when we would go through the agony of trying on swimwear in the department store, I ruled out recycling gently-used thongs. Thongs are also considered butt floss, in case you have not gotten the full picture. Wearing thongs was not a good experience for me! Not comfortable!

Well, I decided to trash them. I very carefully placed them in the tall kitchen trash can under other trash. I didn't want the man of the house to accidently find them! I did this several weeks ago, Chuck, so don't try to find them now. You have already taken them to the dumpster.

Poetry

Ode on a Scrap of Flag *

RICHARD RAYMOND III

South of Poughkeepsie, high on Hudson's shore,
Where the gray towers of West Point arise,
(A bastion of our Revolutionary War,
Target of traitors, goal of Redcoat spies)
There rests a tattered strip of crimson rag
"In honored glory", in a crystal case.
I gazed on what was left of Wainwright's flag
As one who meets a martyr, face to face,
      Blinking back honest tears
To read the news account, now yellowed with the years.

It fluttered, once, above Corregidor,
Where hard-pressed soldiers, sailors, and Marines
Fought hopelessly, yet staunchly all the more,
Knowing what "Duty–Honor–Country" means,
Without relief, respite or resupply.
Beneath a ceaseless rain of bomb and shell
Their Flag still proudly stood against the sky,
As Japanese assailed their citadel.
      Five months crept slowly past,
Then, as they knew it would, the flag came down at last.

Bunker–MacArthur's classmate and close friend–
Performed as duty his most dismal chore,
To haul the flag down at the very end.

Yet, before burning, Colonel Bunker tore
This little corner from a broad red stripe,
Saving its spirit for a better day,
(True soldiers always recognize his type—
A vanished breed, the cynical might say)
Telling his downcast men,
"Take courage, keep the faith—this Flag shall wave again."

Through three long years of harsh captivity
Paul Bunker never wavered in that faith,
That it should rise reborn, aloft and free,
Sustained him to the hour of his death.
Yet he, foreseeing, took a friend aside,
Told Colonel Ausmus of the precious patch
Sewed in his pocket—thus, when Bunker died,
His valiant spirit found a worthy match,
Ausmus survived, to bear
That blood-hued relic back to Freedom's light and air.

In the museum it remains, enshrined,
A silent and unsleeping sentinel,
Warden of West Point spirit, to remind
Gray veterans and young cadets as well,
How gravelly a road is Duty's path;
How Honor can provide a stainless shield;
How Country counts as much as Juice or Math
When prison has become the battlefield.
Rest, soldier, duty done—
May *we* have served as bravely, when our course is run!

---

* One of World War II's most famous slogans was General Douglas MacArthur's pledge "I Shall Return" to the Philippines. Lieutenant General Jona-
than M. Wainwright, MacArthur's successor on Corregidor, had the heartbreak-
ing duty of ordering surrender, when further resistance was impossible. But

in 1945 the compact was fulfilled, when MacArthur stood on the recaptured "Rock", and in ordering a new flag to be raised, warned "let no enemy hand ever lower it". After his repatriation from the prison camp on Formosa, Colonel Delbert Ausmus hand-delivered the little patch to Secretary of War Stimson. He in turn handed it to Bunker's widow, and in due course it was bequeathed to the West Point museum, where I saw it in 1979. It did indeed bring out tears, to read the story.

Poetry

A GARDEN FOR DREAMING LOVERS *

RICHARD RAYMOND III

"... Foole, said my Muse to me, Looke in thy heart, and write."
  - Sidney, "Astrophil and Stella, Sonnet 1"

Saith one who has been long in pallid poems pent,
Getting and spending, laying waste my slender powers,
Gathering fluff for themes, in meters greatly bent,
Tinkering joylessly with idle rhymes, for hours,
"What does it matter, that I labor to invent
Verses which ought to chime from Canterbury's towers?
Not even I can give dead roses back their scent—
Folly indeed, to hope that some may smell the flowers."
Ah—but *these* slips I plant bloom brightly, never dying,
Their petals ever-brilliant, and the rich aroma
Wafts through a window where lovers, linked, are lying,
They smile to sense the sweetness, even in their coma.
And *I* smile, also, touching dim and distant hearts,
Make withered branches blossom, by my mystic arts.

* Sir Philip Sidney (1554 - 86), the very embodiment of Shakespeare's encomium as having "the courtier's, scholar's, soldier's, eye, tongue, sword", composed such a magnificent series of sonnets to his romantic ideal "Stella" (= "Star") that he, imagining himself as Astrophil (= "Star-lover") was one of the brightest among Elizabethan poets. Mortally wounded at the battle of Zutphen, he

is also remembered as having murmured to a fellow-casualty, on declining the offer of a cup of water, "Thy need is greater than mine."

Poetry

"Room For One More" *

RICHARD RAYMOND III

"The verses in it say and say:
'The ones who living come today
To read the stones and go away
Tomorrow dead will come to stay.'"
            - Frost, "In a Disused Graveyard"

Who says our quarter-acre is "disused"?
Stones sprout aplenty, any fool can see,
But years have passed, since mower-blades have cruised
Above us—grass now overtops the knee.
One hundred by one hundred feet, our plot
Contains remains of creatures great and small,
The good, the bad, the doubtful—like as not
There's fine accommodation for you all.
Yes, you, my friend, we stack 'em deep enough
To fit a hundred more, should there be need.
And smaller stones, carved with such silly stuff
As your descendants might delight to read.
No hurry. We'll be waiting, still "in use".
When once we claim you, none shall turn you loose.

* Frost had a lot to say about death. He was probably well acquainted with the old Roman inscription "Memento Mori".

Nonfiction

In the Steps of Jack the Ripper

RICHARD RAYMOND, III

Even after the passage of more than a hundred thirty years, the fogs of East London still obscure the bloody footprints of one of the world's most notorious killers. And to this day, hundreds of chilled thrill-seekers still walk the dim lanes and alleys of his habitat, perhaps hoping—vainly, of course—to winkle out a clue to his identity. So did my wife and I, in the raw spring of 2001, during our vacation sojourn to the British Isles.

Among our chosen tours was an evening's stroll, led by a professional guide, along the scarlet path left by Jack the Ripper, who in the fall of 1888 held all London, especially poor harlots in the streets of Whitechapel, in the grip of terror. Along with some two dozen other tourists, we boarded a bus, and while rolling through the crowded streets harkened to a detailed lecture on the whole series of crimes. There had been other murders in this area, but none so horrific—the most salient feature was the methodical carving-up of the victims: Mary Ann Nichols (age 43), Annie Chapman (47), Elizabeth "Long Liz" Stride (44), Catherine Eddowes (46), and the youngest, most gruesomely-mutilated, Mary Jane Kelly (26). Some reports had it that she had been some four months pregnant; if so, her infant likewise did not survive.

One fascinating aspect of this case—apart from the utter failure of the police to discover the perpetrator—was the series of taunting postcards, ostensibly written by the killer, who signed himself "Jack the Ripper", and boasted of having "fried and eaten" part of one victim's kidney. A major difficulty arose from the fact that the district lay in the purview of two separate agencies, the Metropolitan Police (Scotland Yard) and the City of London

Police. Each had assigned a team of detectives, and the "coopera-tion" between the two often verged on competition.

Sir Charles Warren, the Metropolitan Police Commissioner, in particular demonstrated a singular lack of competence, in that he ordered a chalked message on a nearby wall to be erased, widely believed to have been a clue to the killer. (More of that in due course.) But in the end, as nearly everyone knows, no solution was ever found, and the thousand ingenious speculations by amateur sleuths and clever mystery-writers have served only to keep the case forever open.

So matters stood, when our bus stopped at Buck's Row—since renamed Durward Street—and we disembarked as the guide con-tinued his well-practiced spiel. It was a dark evening, rather chilly, and the hint of mist in the air did nothing to dispel the gloom of that dreary neighborhood. During the Second World War, Lon-don's East End had been hard-hit by German bombs, and after the war vast areas of shattered buildings had been cleared away and entire districts largely rebuilt. Hence it rather distracted from the old-time atmosphere when our guide was obliged to describe a modern warehouse, currently in business use, as the spot where the unhappy Ms Nichols was found, throat cut and otherwise bad-ly dealt with.

All five murders had taken place within a few blocks of one another, and the best guess that police detectives could derive was that the killer lived nearby—a supposition that latter-day authors have scornfully derided. Nonetheless, our little group proceeded on foot, as did Jack and his unwitting prey, to visit in succession the one-time haunts of wretched streetwalkers, drink-sodden derelicts who hoped to earn a few pennies to buy them a night's lodging in a filthy and bug-ridden "doss-house." At length we arrived at the "Ten Bells", a pub at which, so tradition has it, Jack himself may have sipped a pint of stout, while scanning the clientele for a likely prospect. It's been modernized, of course, with electric lighting and heating, which somehow fails to overcome its ancient sleazi-ness, and, if you squint your eyes, a bit of atmosphere.

But now, after pausing for a slug of mild-and-bitter, we returned to our mournful safari and stood at last on the ground floor of a great big concrete parking garage. This, our guide explained, was all that remained of Number 13 Miller's Court, the grubby domicile of the late Mary Jane Kelly, whose shredded corpse was discovered one November morning in her overheated room. Jack had had ample time and privacy for full play with his snickersnee.

Following this, and with a wary glance around, we reboarded the bus and made good speed back to the warmth and cheer of our hotel. Among the many remarks by passengers in reaction to our excursion were these: "How could those poor drabs have allowed him to get so close?" and "Why did no one scream for help?" But according to police reports, only one did—the late Mary Jane Kelly who was said to have cried "Murder!" in her last extremity. And really, how else would a homely old tramp attempt to lure a customer but by cozying up to him?

***

Without going into a lot of detail in consideration of these events, I may state that I did read some of the published works by an assortment of authors, scholars, and students of sensational true crime. The list is long, and even at this late date, more books are appearing on the subject, which seems to exert an endless fascination for writers. And despite the fervent claims of certain ones, the mystery has never been definitively concluded. This keeps alive the tantalizing prospect that a final answer may lie in the future.

The police questioned more than two thousand persons in their efforts to find the Ripper. Most could be dismissed without further inquiry, having failed the familiar test of Means-Motive-Opportunity. Of the remainder, serious conflicts in motive or opportunity are part of the enduring enigma surrounding the murders. Some of those who write of it—a few almost fanatical in advancing their arguments—insist that the Jews, or the Freemasons, or some political group, must have done it.

As a matter of record, Sir Charles Warren, the Police Commissioner, when he viewed a crudely-chalked message on a wall near one corpse, ordered it to be erased, without even a photograph. It read "The Juwes are the men That Will not be blamed for nothing"—a sentiment which, he feared, might have inflamed public feelings to attack members of London's large Jewish population. Among many other clues was the medical examiner's report that, contrary to newspaper accounts, the mutilations did not require a great deal of skill in anatomy and dissection, even that of a journeyman butcher.

All this being said, let's look at two of the books which particularly interested me, offering diametrically opposed views of the killer. The first was *Murder and Madness: The Secret Life of Jack the Ripper,* by Dr. David Abrahamsen, MD, a forensic psychoanalyst whose interviews of the "Son of Sam" killer stirred much controversy. The second was *Portrait of a Killer: Jack the Ripper, Case Closed,* by novelist Patricia Cornwell.

Abrahamsen had earned a medical degree in his native Norway, and, after many years' practice in Great Britain, moved to the United States, where he continued his work of investigating the criminal mind. Among his other publications is *Confessions of Son of Sam* (1985), based on lengthy conversations with the serial killer in his prison. He believed, with reason, in the guilt of a man few would have credited with such a string of butcheries—James Kenneth Stephen, second son of a justice.

He was a brilliant scholar, poet, and author who served as tutor to Prince Albert Victor, eldest son of Edward, Prince of Wales, and a grandson of Queen Victoria. Those reasons will be remarked on in due course.

Ms Cornwell, for her part, has achieved much success with her cleverly-woven tales of mayhem and murder, including twenty-four books in her "Kay Scarpetta, Medical Examiner" series and four non-fiction books, including *Portrait of a Killer.* In a word, she has become comfortably well-off and does not hesitate to express herself on subjects far distant from pathology. She firmly maintains that Jack was really Walter Sickert, a noted British artist, some of whose paintings bear disturbing images which might possibly indicate a diseased mind.

Having gained a wide reputation as mystery writer, her conclusions are based on some very expensive research—she claims to have spent over seventeen million dollars in her hunt for the Ripper.

In that pursuit, she went so far as to purchase some thirty of Sickert's paintings, subjecting them to intense scrutiny and even destroying one in an attempt to capture a sample of his DNA, hoping to find a match with the saliva from one of Jack's nasty postcards.

As to the artist himself, he was alleged to have had some abnormality of the genitals, possibly enough to be the cause of murderous rages. If true, it does not appear to have affected his marital ventures, for he married three times, and during the Whitechapel murders was still married to his first wife. But alas for Ms. Cornwell, more than one slaying took place when Sickert was known to have been in France.

The burden of what she regards as proof seems to rest largely on the supposed similarity of his "Camden Town Murder" paintings with the horrid scene in Kelly's bedroom. She also noted that the watermarks on Sickert's note paper match those on the Ripper letters. But such stationery had been widely sold and might easily have been used by both. Ms. Cornwell's analysis has received severe rebuke from a number of critics who studied the case more thoroughly than she. If in fact she spent such a sum in her inquiry, it may have been wasted. More significant, in my view, is the complete omission of any mention of Abrahansen's 1992 book in her bibliography. She simply ignored a contrary opinion, though it was readily available through libraries. The same is true of other authors' views.

All in all, I found her analysis far from convincing, and I once more turned to Abrahamsen for a different slant. In surfing through a number of websites treating with his book, I came across one review site called "Casebook", in which the reviewer positively scorched the notion that either Stephen or the Prince could possibly have been the culprit(s). In the words of one website comment, "Abrahamsen suspected that Prince Albert Victor and James Kenneth Stephen worked as a collaborating team to commit the Jack the Ripper murders." And in truth, much of Abrahamsen's "evidence" does depend heavily on internal, psychological reading. But that is what he, as a certified professional, was qualified to perform.

And it is undeniable that young Stephen—scion of a distinguished family (and incidentally first cousin to author Virginia Woolf, whom he was suspected to have molested as a child) and son of a Royal Judge—was vehemently unfond of women and, in all probability, was a practicing homosexual. In school at Eton and later King's College, Cambridge, he was known for his powerful physique and excellence in vigorous sports. As a graduate, he was appointed official tutor to the Prince, whom Abrahamsen asserted became his boy-lover. In the England of that time, such activities were contrary to law—as Oscar Wilde learned, to his sorrow—so the circle of his acquaintances was kept very much in the shadows.

In addition to his other psychological and medical conditions, he had suffered a severe blow to the cranium, an accident which either brought on or worsened a growing siege of bipolarity. He was capable of composing the most charming and witty poetry, alternating with furious rages, which given his size and strength were most dangerous. Was this enough to have turned him to murder? Abrahamsen thought so, for this was the theme of *Murder and Madness*.

As a sample of his views on the female sex, I append one of his sprightly little verses, leaving it to the reader to ponder whether it betokens darker passions.

"That lanky hank of a she in the inn over there
Nearly killed me for asking the loan of a glass of beer,
May the Devil grip the whey-face slut by the hair
And beat bad manners out of her skin for a year."
"That parboiled ape, with the toughest jaw you will see
On virtue's path, and voice that would rasp the dead,
Came roaring and raging the moment she looked at me,

And threw me out of the house on the back of my head.
If I asked her master, he'd give me a cask a day,
But she, with the gallons at hand, not a gill would
      arrange—
May she marry a ghost and bear him a kitten, and may
The High King of Glory permit her to get the mange."

Now to return to the "Juwes" message. Is it so far out of reason to imagine that it may have been—to pinch Holmes' canny
term—a "blind", deliberately using misspelling and crude grammar to conceal the hand of a well-educated man, quick, strong,
and ruthless in his savagery? For he did slay two in a single night, a
few streets apart, which led investigators to conclude he may have
been interrupted in the first.

So there you have it. On the one hand, Cornwell plumps for
Sickert, on the other, Abrahamsen says Stephen, possibly abetted
by "Prince Eddy" as lookout during his mad moments. Not coin-
cidentally, the doctor points out, all the murders took place during
holidays from Cambridge and within a short walk from a connecting railway line. It's a matter of incontrovertible fact that, within
a few days of the death—purportedly from "pneumonia"—of
Prince Eddy, Stephen went into a black chasm of depression.
While confined in a mental institution, he refused to eat and, in
this state of melancholia, starved himself to death. From that day,
there had been no more butchered bawds in back alleys.

No *solid* evidence? Bosh! I have *poetic* evidence, to me even
more convincing than that of smug scholars and amateur sleuths.
Such as can arise only in the mind of an accomplished poet and
inveterate punster, whose eye can pierce the obfuscating veil of
foggy speculation and arrive at THE TRUTH!

One of the unremarked-on facets of young Stephen's character was his penchant for paranomasia, or witty puns. Consider
the following verse, which caused many critics to smile, written in
response to the literary pretensions of H. Rider Haggard (author
of "She" and "King Solomon's Mines", etc.) and Rudyard Kipling
(author of "Kim", "The Jungle Books", etc.)

"To R. K.

Will there never come a season
Which shall rid us from the curse
Of a prose which knows no reason
And an unmelodious verse;
When the world shall cease to wonder
At the genius of an Ass,
And a boy's eccentric blunder
Shall not bring success to pass;
When mankind shall be delivered
From the clash of magazines,
And the inkstand shall be shivered
Into countless smithereens;
When there stands a muzzled stripling
Mute, beside a muzzled bore,
When the Rudyards cease from Kipling,
And the Haggards Ride no more.?"

Applying the diamond-hard logic of the fictional Sherlock Holmes, I affirm that such sentiments can only arise from a mind at once brilliantly and tragically, criminally warped. And without for a moment confessing to the possession of such faculties, I instantly grasped the significance of the mad killer's selection of the name "JACK" in his merciless guying of the bumbling police detectives.

He was deliberately giving a broad hint as to his identity, which in their stolid, humorless fashion, entirely escaped the comprehension of the London cops. As a polished classical scholar, Stephen was perfectly conversant in several languages, among them Greek, Latin, and French. Now, take a look at this: Jack = Jacques (French) = James, aka JAMES KENNETH STEPHEN. QED.

What could be clearer? Once the code is broken, Abrahamsen's thesis is proved, to the discomfiture and overthrow of the peacock-popinjay novelist.

I rest my case.

Fiction

Little Scout Lost

RICHARD RAYMOND III

"What in tarnation is that kind of crazy name, "Hungry Mother State Park"? the retired Botetourt County sheriff demanded to know, "and why didn't someone feed her?"

Flora, Renard's silver-haired wife of nearly sixty years, chuckled tolerantly. "Good thing you can hardly see to read the rest of this sign, Ervin," she said. "It would drive you even crazier. Listen to this: 'The Legend of Hungry Mother. In 1757, when Indians raided and destroyed several settlements along New River, Molly Marley and her small child were among the captives. They were taken to the Indians' encampment, but later escaped, to wander through the wilderness, eating only berries. Molly finally collapsed, and the child wandered on down the creek until she found help. All she could say was 'Hungry ... Mother'. The rescue party arrived at the mountain-top to find Molly lying dead of starvation and fatigue. Today the mountain is called 'Molly's Knob', and the stream is 'Hungry Mother Creek'. Now isn't that a pretty little story?"

"Hmph," grunted the sheriff, "Well, if *I* had been leading that rescue party..."

"As blind as you mostly are," replied Flora drily, "you'd have been twice as lost. And wild berries give you the indigestion. But now let's try to find some pretty things at the arts and crafts show. We also have to stop by Elaine McIver's watercolor exhibit—she's sure to win a prize for her beautiful paintings. There's ever so much to do, and if *you* get hungry, Lord knows you'll eat. This place is packed with refreshment stands."

It was nearing noon on Saturday, July 20, 1974, at the state park a few miles north of Marion, Va. Ervin and Flora Renard had accepted the kind invitation of their old friends Dr. and Mrs. Paul McIver to attend the fair, and the good doctor had driven the little party down from Fincastle the night before, staying for the weekend at a Holiday Inn. Now they were enjoying themselves, wandering down the aisles between the exhibitors' booths, stopping now and then to watch a craftsman at work.

Of a sudden they became aware of a thunder of engines, as a long convoy of trucks and cars began to arrive in the parking lot near the crafts tents. Under direction of a park ranger, the vehicles lined up in column and immediately started to disembark scores of men and boys, County sheriff's deputies, state police, Boy Scout leaders with their troops, and a swarm of other men, all dressed for rough walking. In double-quick time, the newcomers were formed into sections and marched briskly up the hill to the Hemlock Haven Conference Center, where they were strung out into long skirmish lines. The visitors were astonished. "What's happening?" asked Renard, "I hear a lot of trucks and such. Sounds like a mob coming in."

Flora plucked at the sleeve of a passing ranger. "Please, sir," she inquired, "what's all the excitement?"

The ranger paused. "Bad news, ma'am. There's a Cub Scout missing from a weekend camping trip, and we've got to find him. Gets right cold up here, even in summer, and a storm front's moving in. No time to waste. 'Scuse me now, gotta run." And he trotted off in the wake of the marching column.

"My gosh," exclaimed Renard, "that really does sound bad. I've had the unhappy duty of leading at least a dozen such searches for lost hikers in the hills around Fincastle, and half of them ended in tragedy. Lots of places to fall down a mountainside, with bears and poisonous snakes and what-all out there. Isn't there anything we can do? Can't we go up to where those fellows are getting their orders? We've got Doc McIver here. Surely his medical kit would come in handy."

"Ervin," sighed his wife, "as dim-sighted as you are and as old as we all are, don't imagine we'd be of much use. Wait a minute, here comes someone who could give us some information."

The "someone" was a little sparrow of a woman, clad in the distinctive yellow blouse, blue kerchief, and slacks of a Cub Scout leader, hurrying toward them up the path, her face a study of anxiety, literally wringing her hands with worry. "Oh dear, oh dear," she was murmuring, "whatever shall we do? I'll never forgive myself if any harm's come to Kenny."

Flora swung round to block her path. "Ma'am," she began kindly, "you've got some trouble on your mind. This is Sheriff Renard, of Botetourt County, I'm his wife, Flora, and here is Doctor Paul McIver, who was County Medical Examiner before he retired some years ago. We've done some searches in the past and haven't forgotten how. Please let us help."

The woman stopped, mouth open with astonishment, then bravely tried to stanch her tears. "Oh, thank you, thank you, but I don't know what else to do. I'm Hetty Twitchell, the Webelos' den mother, and little Kenny Houchin is one of my Cubs. A dozen Webelos were on a weekend camp-out with my husband, Tom, the Cubmaster, and three of the fathers. They were on a nature walk yesterday afternoon, and along the trail someone stepped on a yellowjackets' nest. Well, you just know they all scattered like birdshot, with the stinging bugs in hot pursuit. It took almost half an hour to get the boys reassembled, and Kenny was not among them.

"No one had seen which way he ran, and after searching and calling till sundown, they came back down and reported to the park ranger. The sheriff organized a big search party overnight. They're up there now, trying to find him. Oh, Lordy, what can I say to his mother—she's my dearest friend!" And she began again to weep.

Flora was a no-nonsense type. "Crying won't find anyone," she replied crisply. "Can you guide us to where the boys were when they scattered?"

Hetty Twitchell gulped and made a stout-hearted effort. "W-w-well, I-I think so. My husband told me. It's just up that trail yonder."

"Then let's be at it," commanded Flora, and they began to ascend the path. It was a matter of some thirty minutes before the little group stood under a huge sycamore at the peak of the hill, gazing uncertainly about. They could still hear the line of searchers, pushing through the thick brush and calling loudly for the lost scout. Hetty looked down the trail. "I...I *think* this is where Tom said they were. And right over there I can see a couple of bees or something buzzing around."

"Well," Flora remarked, "as a practical matter, we ought not to just wander like Molly the Hungry Mother. And I'm convinced that those fellows are going in the wrong direction. Call it Scot's Instinct. Let's start here and continue down the path, *avoiding* that nest. Ouch!"

Renard and McIver were all concern. "Did something sting you?"

Flora had reached down to rub her aching toe. "No, some idiot left a pile of rocks just where folks could stumble over it." Hetty was on her knees in a moment.

"Why, it's a scout sign!" she exclaimed excitedly. "Three flat stones in a stack, with another on the ground, to point the way to follow. Somebody has given us a clue!"

"If it's a trail, let's follow it," suggested the sheriff.

"Not so fast, dear," Flora put in. "I think it would be better if you stood right here to mark the spot, and if we find anything down there to give a signal. Do you still carry your police whistle?"

"Always," he said. "In this cool air, the sound should carry far."

With that, Flora, Hetty and McIver walked cautiously at right angles to the trail, ducking through the underbrush as best they might. Flora spotted something fluttering in the light breeze, just ahead. "Oh-ho, what's *that*?" Quickly stepping to the trunk of a large oak tree, she pointed to the haft of a pocketknife, stabbed deeply into the bark about three feet above the ground, and bearing a strip of what seemed to be dirty whitish cloth.

"If it's a trail marker," she ventured, "there should be another, just...about...*there*!" With a laugh, she pushed ahead to where a second cloth strip was tied to the end of a twig. Thus they proceeded for nearly half a mile, until they came to the edge of a steep ravine

Flora paused for breath. "Oof! I hope we don't have to climb down there! But I can't see any more...wait! Look, at the bottom, just under that pile of pine branches, is that an arm and hand? It is! It moved! Hetty, can you get us down without breaking our necks?" It meant a lengthy detour, but the three at last stood beside the stack of greenery, hurriedly throwing the branches aside and calling anxiously, "Kenny, Kenny, is that you?" And so it was.

***

Sheriff Renard had been waiting for more than an hour under the sycamore, and his own anxiety increased with every passing minute. But his hearing was keener than ever, and his vision, so dim after the terrible explosion at Norfolk, over twenty years before, was yet sufficient to see an approaching figure. His heart was immeasurably gladdened to hear and view the yellow-and-blue shape of Hetty Twitchell, puffing with the effort of her steep climb.

"Sheriff! Sheriff!" she cried as soon as she had breath, "He's down there, in a terrible ravine. Flora and the doctor are with him. He's badly hurt, ankle broken, all bumps and bruises, almost delirious with fever, but alive! He's alive. Doctor says he'll be all right, by and by! Blow your whistle! Let the search party know we've found him!" And Renard began to blast on the brass whistle with all his might.

The next two hours were filled with busy activity, as half a dozen sturdy troopers and deputies made their way down to the fallen scout, quickly cut a pair of poles, and used two jackets to make an improvised stretcher. With this, they managed with difficulty to carry young Kenny up to the crest and back along the path to Hemlock Haven and safety. Flora, Hetty, Renard, and the doctor trailed along behind, quietly discussing with a State Police sergeant some of the puzzling aspects of this rescue.

"Sergeant," said Flora, thoughtfully rubbing her chin, "there's things about this that I don't think should be discussed outside of ourselves, who were there. After Paul had given the boy a shot to lessen the pain, he and I had a chance to talk with the brave little fellow, and this truly borders on the occult. As he said, when the yellowjackets started after them, he and the others took off in all directions, as fast as they could run, anywhere away from that swarm. He darted through the bushes and didn't know where he was until he fetched up on the edge of that ravine. Tried to stop, tripped on a root, and down he went, bashing himself up pretty well and breaking his ankle.

She paused, and her eyes narrowed. "Okay, now follow this. He was semi-conscious, alone, lost, hurt, immobilized. And who should come along, about evening, but a little girl, maybe five-six years old, said he. Now I tell it as he told us, something hardly believable, except for the physical evidence. Stuff like this." She placed in his hands a half-dozen strips of cloth, about one inch wide and twelve long, "They marked the trail to the boy. I pulled them off some trees and bushes as we returned with the stretcher bearers. Hetty, would you tell him what these are?"

The den mother's voice was low, almost trembling. "I manage a fabric shop in Marion. I know materials. These swatches are blue check cotton gingham. It was once popular in the colonies, but this type hasn't been woven for nearly two hundred years. I have no idea how they came to be here. Now, today."

Flora persisted. "And where did we find the first one?"

"It was tied around the belt loop of Kenny's scout knife. Stuck in the tree. And the bark had grown up around the blade. Almost covered, up to the handle. Must have been there for...I can't guess how many years."

The sergeant scratched his head in wonderment. "How'd you know it was his? There's a million Scout knives out there."

Hetty stammered, "B-b-but it had to be, it had his name on it! All our boys have to label their property." She lapsed into stunned silence.

"Doctor," Flora continued, "what did he tell you while we

waited for the stretcher?"

McIver laconically replied, "He said the little girl, gave her name as Abby, looked a mess. Ragged blue-check dress, barefoot, leaves and twigs in her tangled hair, spoke in a strange fashion, seemed like a lost child herself. But she used his pocket-knife to cut a pile of pine branches and cover him against the cold. Stayed with him through the night, didn't seem to feel the chill, brought him water from the creek, said she'd mark a trail.

"Come daylight, told him she had to go see her Mama. 'But dinna fash yersel', 'ye'll be fund anon.' That she said, he was certain. Last he saw, she was walking up the creekside, with a handful of strips she cut from the hem of her frock. Next thing he knew, we were there. That's all. Make of it what you can."

Flora said slowly, with emphasis. "*Fash*, you may know, Sergeant, is an old Scots expression, meaning vex or worry. No one these days would use it. And wasn't Molly Marley of Highland stock? Coincidence? Make a guess. Some questions, I surmise, will find no easy answers. Who was the girl? Where did she come from? Where did she go? How could a little child prove to be so handy in the woods? The Houchin boy was sure he didn't tell her how to make a scout trail marker. Be interesting to find the name of that lost Marley child–if it turns out to be Abby, you're only a step from the 'Twilight Zone'."

Renard could not refrain from adding, "And Flora knew, just *knew*, the searchers were going in the wrong direction. She put us on the track. I couldn't see, but she did, and clearly."

The sergeant stopped, staring at her. "If I tell this to the captain, he'll put me in the Marion asylum. What do I say?"

Flora laughed. "Why tell him anything? The boy was found. He will be on crutches for a while but should make a good recovery. If your captain presses you, just say the sheriff had a hunch. He'll understand that."

"*Your* hunch, you mean," replied the sergeant with a grin.

She laughed again, wholeheartedly, "Och, Ser'eant, dinna ye ken, all wee Scots lassies ha' the Second Sight!"

And the four visitors ambled off down the path, leaving the

trooper with a few gingham strips and a great mystery on his
hands.

Nonfiction

The Right Place at the Right Time

SALLY ROSEVEARE (POSTHUMOUS)

On a tall pole on Smith Mountain Lake's shore sits a large nest with a pair of ospreys. Smart folks at Smith Mountain Lake State Park attached a video camera to the nest and connected the video to a TV monitor inside the Welcome Center. This allows interested people to watch live, happening-right-this-moment action in the nest.

Ron and I took college friends to see these fascinating raptors. Inside the Welcome Center, we watched the male and female tend their three eggs. The female, larger than the male, spread her wings and flew away. The male checked the eggs and rearranged the nesting material. He looked like a typical proud daddy.

As we watched, the middle egg cracked, and a chick struggled out of the shell. Excited, I snapped pictures. Then the egg on the left cracked, and another chick emerged. By now I was almost jumping up and down. I could have watched all day.

Even though they didn't turn out very well, I took pictures. Lots of them. Fifty-one, to be exact. Technical people would know why the photos weren't great. All I know is that there were lots of wavy lines across the screen. I hope you can get an idea of what transpired.

Ten minutes later, Momma returned with a stick approximately 24 inches long. She put the stick on the edge of the nest, didn't like it there, and tried tucking it in a couple more spots.

We laughed. She was "rearranging the furniture." Daddy refused to move away from the newly-hatched chicks. We laughed again as Momma turned and whopped him in the head with the stick. Was it accidental or on purpose? Anyhow, Daddy moved. Momma put the stick down, examined her babies, and tore meat off a dead fish stashed in the nest. After eating, she regurgitated and fed them. From what I've read, the parents will feed chicks for three months.

When the babies were eight days old, I checked on their progress. Larger now, they were in shadows, not easily visible. I took pictures anyhow. I'll return weekly to see how they're doing. And I'll continue taking pictures. I feel close to this osprey family. I pray none of them will get tangled on fishing line or any of the trash some humans discard with no thought to what their actions cost our critters.

And I give thanks for being in the right place at the right time. And with my camera, too!

"The Right Place at the right Time" appeared on Sally's blog, *Smith Mountain Lake Mystery Writer*, on May 28, 2008.

Fiction

Grocery Shopping Could Be Fun!

SALLY ROSEVEARE (POSTHUMOUS)

I detest grocery shopping. I do it only because eating is one of the few things I excel in. (I never met a potato I didn't like—or hardly any other food dish, for that matter, nuts included.) I don't like comparison-shopping the grocery flyers, I don't like the 25-plus-minute drive to the nearest grocery store, and I'd rather be in my kayak or writing at my computer. To me, grocery shopping is just plain boring.

But guess what! I've come up with ways to make grocery shopping an enjoyable experience. And if the stores played it right, they could increase their revenue. How could this be accomplished? Well . . .

Monthly cart of competitions:

1. I've always wanted to use a grocery cart as a scooter. I've thought about this for eons. Cart competition would work this way. Using those orange traffic cones, the grocery store would set up an obstacle course in the parking lot (away from customers' vehicles, of course). Each competitor would select a cart, receive a can of WD-40 and a rag, and be allowed 10 minutes to oil the cart's wheels and make other adjustments. At the appointed time, each competitor would hold onto his/her cart handle, put one foot on the metal bar near the bottom of the cart, and push off

with the other foot. (The push-off foot could push as often as desired.) Of course each entry would be clocked, with seconds added on for each time one of the cones was clipped or missed. This event could mushroom into a big deal. Preliminary competition could start on the city/town level, then countywide, statewide, and national. The national winner could receive a year's supply of groceries, a new hybrid car or pick-up truck, or maybe a vacation to Hawaii along with a copy of my book *Secrets at Spawning Run*.

2. Ever wonder how many stacked-behind-each-other carts one grocery store employee can guide through a parking lot? I want to know! In this cart competition, the grocery store would have each department, e.g., meat, produce, beverage, dairy, deli, etc., choose a worker from their respective department. Or maybe all employees would be eligible if they wished. That would depend on the individual store. Willing employees would put their cart-guiding prowess to work after training for 15 minutes. The winner would receive a stainless steel trophy in the shape of, well, a grocery cart. A package of T-bone steaks, and Popeye's favorite—canned spinach—would also be won! This competition could also go national.

3. Because little kids are adorable and draw big crowds, there would be an event for them, too. Besides, the kids' parents and other relatives would come to watch and cheer their little darlings to victory—and spend lots of money at the store. The children would use the child-sized grocery carts we've all dodged numerous times. Parents would be given 10 minutes to decorate their children's buggies with items purchased at the store. Each child would race a cart through the store's aisles while trying not to hit cardboard cutout persons with carts popping up unexpectedly. Along the way, the child would be required to pick up a product from each aisle. Groceries knocked off the shelves by runaway carts would count against the contestant. I suggest that all competitors be timed the way a downhill slalom skier is timed so that they wouldn't ram each

other, cry, and cause fighting among the parents. Also, helmets would be required. The winner—and all losers—would receive the same prizes. (It would never do for one child to receive more than the others. We certainly don't want kids to think they need to excel in order to receive prizes.) This could be a national competition, too, but we don't want any child's feelings hurt, so maybe not.

At each of the above competitions, the deli would sell sandwiches, drinks, and other goodies.

Dancing in the aisles:

How many times have you wanted to cha-cha to the sounds of 40s music, bop to 50s music, and shag to Carolina beach music, all playing on the grocery stores' speakers? Sometimes it takes every bit of my will power to resist; a couple of times I couldn't control myself. A few years ago I was stared at when I did a few cha-cha steps in the canned foods aisle. "Cherry Pink and Apple Blossom White" by Perez Prado was playing. This year when I heard "Under the Boardwalk" by the Drifters, I scurried to the produce department and squeezed in a few shagging steps in the aisle between the apples and the avocados before another shopper intruded. But the overwhelming desire to really "break out" still persists. Here is what I propose:

Grocery stores could set aside a small area (probably best not near the wine display) of perhaps 15 x 20 feet for those who are moved (literally) by a catchy tune. If customers preferred doing a two-step as they pushed their carts down the aisles, then that would be okay, too. In fact, this should be encouraged. I believe shoppers would stay in the stores longer—they wouldn't want to stop dancing to a great beat until the song ended. Therefore, they'd spend more money. I visualize dance lovers stopping by the grocery store on the way home from an evening meeting in order to end the night on a relaxing note. Diners who've just feasted on a delicious restaurant meal would stop by, too. Cheap guys who promised their dates a night of dinner and dancing would also drop in. The bakery department could have four-tiered cakes ready to ice with the appropriate romantic inscription on top at a moment's notice. And the possibilities for wedding receptions are endless!

So talk to your grocery store manager and get his/her opinion. And please let me know where you think I will enjoy grocery shopping!

"Grocery Shopping Could Be Fun!" originally appeared on Sally's blog in October 2006.

Fiction

Breakfast with My Family

LINDA KAY SIMMONS

I awake to the smell of apple pie baking in the oven. I pull back my many covers and get out of bed. Looking at my clock, I see it is five a.m. Who was baking a pie at this time of the morning? No one has a key to my house but my daughter, Noelle, and she is in Kentucky. My darling girl is surprising me with a visit and an early breakfast! She knows how I love to eat apple pie for any meal, but why didn't Spike bark when she came in? That isn't like him. Even now he lies with his head on a pillow.

"Some watchdog you are, Spike," I say to my little guy, a chihuahua and dachshund mix. I throw a robe over my nightgown and go downstairs to the kitchen, all prepared to give my daughter a huge hug, but it isn't she!

My mother, grandmother, and Aunt Ramona are sitting at the table drinking tea from my special china cups. An elderly lady, wearing a brown hat with three owl feathers, is sitting with them. The four women turn and smile at me. I feel my eyes grow large as saucers.

"It's so good of you to wake up and join us this morning, Linda. So often you don't," Grandmother says. "It's about time."

"About time? What do you mean? I've never seen you in my kitchen before! I'm just a bit startled to see all of you, not that I'm not thrilled to have you in my home," I say, wanting everyone to feel welcome.

"Linda, sweetheart, we are often in your kitchen. We like having tea at this table. We have some of our best times here," Mama replies as she reaches across the table for a slice of lemon.

"The table makes it easier for us to come in," Grandmother

says, smiling pleasantly. "It holds such special memories. Your grandfather Elbert and I bought it when we set up housekeeping in 1918. I raised Elizabeth and Ramona at this table, and you ate many meals on it as a little girl. I'm delighted you wanted to keep it. It's so welcoming. It's one of the reasons I like coming here. I so like spending time with Elizabeth and Ramona and getting caught up with what's going on in your life."

"Linda's always been a sweet girl. People thought she looked like me when she was a baby and took her for mine," Aunt Ramona says, looking at me and laughing. "She's taken after me in more ways than one."

"She has had her moments," Mama replies as she adds water to the tea kettle, attempting to change the conversation.

"Mama used to get mad at me when I was a teenager and would tell me I was just like you, Aunt Ramona. I took it as a compliment because Mama and Daddy's life was so boring. I'm so glad to see you here. I've missed you," I say, wondering how all of this had come about.

Mama waves her hand, dismissing my conversation with Aunt Ramona. "Sewing wild oats is what they called it in my day."

"I'm glad I enjoyed myself when I could because look where we are now," Ramona says, gesturing wildly with her arms. Mama rolls her eyes, and I can tell their sibling rivalry is still going strong.

"Hey, I'm right here," I say. "Remember me?"

"We know you are, dear. It's just the way we communicate," Grandmother answers, as she peers at me over her bifocals.

"I'm just surprised to find you all here in my kitchen. I think I'd better get a glass of water and sit down," I say as I fill my glass at the sink.

"You shouldn't be surprised, Linda. We hear you talking to us as you go through your day, and we all like what you've done to your writing area, hanging all the special pictures of us on the walls," Mama says, her blue eyes twinkling. "It's just how I would have done it."

"So you've been through my whole house?" I ask, feeling embarrassed. "Do you see everything?"

"Heavens, yes, dear. We can go anywhere, particularly when we've been invited," Mama says.

"While you're up, Linda, get the pie out of the oven. I'm sure it's ready by now. It smells delicious. Please use my china plates," Grandmother instructs me as she fusses with one of her pin curls. I smile, remembering her using blue rinse on her hair when I was little, and from the looks of her she still does.

"And my silver forks," Mama tells me. "They should be in the silver chest."

"It' so nice Linda is sentimental about our things, isn't it? And she's kept so many of them. It's good to be around familiar objects," Grandmother says, her eyes moist with tears.

I busy myself getting the plates from the china cabinet in the dining room and the forks from the silver chest I keep in the kitchen closet. I take the plates and forks to the kitchen and place them on the table.

"Linda always was one for valuing our treasured items," Grandmother says, as she picks up a plate and examines it. "I've always liked this pattern, *The Eaton*, with the lovely birds and gold rims."

"Hopefully, Noelle will too, and everything will continue to be passed down," Mother says, speaking as if I weren't there.

"Mama, I don't want to be rude, but I'd like to talk to the lady sitting at the table with you," I say, looking at the familiar-looking woman as she gently fingers the owl feathers on her hat.

"Oh, we have been chattering like magpies. Linda, this is Sara Bernstein," Mama says as she cuts the pie into large pieces, dropping a piece on the floor and causing the others to giggle.

"Welcome to my home, Mrs. Bernstein," I say, gulping hard. "It's so nice to be with you again."

"Do you remember several months ago, while you were in deep meditation and asking for a writing muse, your Grandfather Elbert and I showed up for you?" Mrs. Bernstein asks. "I wasn't wearing this hat the day you came. I just got it, especially for today. What do you think?"

"Your hat is lovely. I think the owl feathers threw me when I first saw you. But now I remember everything about our visit.

Your home in Germany is lovely, and I was so surprised to see my grandfather sitting with you in your kitchen. I knew who he was immediately from old photographs. I felt so close to him when we talked. It was like I had known him my entire life. The day after our visit, I read about your life in *The Seamstress*. I downloaded it on Amazon. The book moved me to tears. You are a very brave lady, Mrs. Bernstein."

"Thank you, Linda. That's very sweet of you. You know, we can meet anytime you like," she said. "It isn't difficult."

"I'd like that, Mrs. Bernstein."

Grandmother coughed. I could tell she wanted to speak without being overly rude by interrupting us. "Elbert was a good husband and father, even though his life was cut short. I'm so glad you spent time with him, Linda. He told me it meant the world to him." Turning her attention to Mrs. Bernstein, Grandmother continued, "Isn't it peculiar I was a seamstress, as was my sister, Mamie? I took in sewing when Elbert died at 49, and I had Elizabeth and Ramona to raise."

"I've found there are never any coincidences," Mrs. Bernstein says, turning her attention to me. "Linda, do you see how all of this is weaving together?"

"I'm beginning to, Mrs. Bernstein. Is that why you are here— to help me with my next book?"

"Yes, dear. We were all talking about that just before you came downstairs. I'm going to let your grandmother pick up the conversation from here."

"Linda, we might as well get to the point. We've come here to discuss your writing. We want you to listen to what we have to say. You may not know it," Grandmother says smiling, "but I have always wanted to write. I remember when you found the ballad I wrote called 'Little Jim' in the family Bible and how it made you cry when you read it. You didn't know I was watching you, but I was. Would you mind bringing that Bible downstairs and leaving it on the table for our next visit, dear?"

"Of course I don't mind; I can get it now if you want," I say, rising from the table.

"Our next visit will be soon enough," Grandmother says. "We still have much to discuss. It's your mother's turn to talk now."

Mama clears her throat before she begins to talk, and I wonder if she is going to be long-winded.

"When you were growing up, Linda, you watched me try to write romance novels on my Remington typewriter. I never got far, but oh how I wanted to write. I never could stick with it. I'm so proud of you for writing two novels. I know it was hard work," Mama says, smiling at me with pride.

"Mama, you always read to me when I was little. My favorite times were going to the library with you. Remember how you had me write little books and you'd make library cards to put in the back? You had an ink pad and stamper, just like the librarian. Daddy and Aunt Mamie would check out my books and return them to my collection by the due date. I did that for Noelle when she was little, but you were around for that. You remember checking out her books, don't you?"

"Of course I do. I remember everything now," Mama says, reaching her hands out and taking mine.

"It was you, Mama, who taught me to love reading and gave me the desire to write," I say, my voice cracking with emotion.

Mama beamed. "You are welcome, my darling girl. Now let's get serious and talk about why we are all here. Linda, you wrote *Cahas Mountain,* which is about your father's side of the family. Even in *Struck By Lightning* it was his side of the family that showed up. We are here to tell you that the Ferguson side of your family wants in on this next book, and we are going to help you write *Lamb On The Tombstone.*"

"Writing a book is like being a seamstress," Mrs. Bernstein chimes in. "First you get a thought, and then a pattern begins to form in your head. Designing with words takes you to all kinds of places, and before you know it, you are cutting scenes from the fabric of life. I particularly like stitching stories together, with little details and different-colored threads, and embroidering for beauty and texture."

"I never thought of it that way, but you are quite right. I imag-

Encore

ine that's why we are all here; each of us wants to send Linda our thoughts and ideas," Mama announces, and the other ladies nod.

"So, Linda, do what you have been doing. Take long meditative walks. We particularly like it when you walk down Rolling Road to the small cemetery. It seems you are very open then and we can give you our best ideas. Sitting at your desk by candlelight makes it easy for us to come to you, too. Now there is something else I have to say because I am your mother. I don't frown on your having a glass or two of red wine while you write; just don't let it get excessive. You know, your character Nettie in your new book has quite a problem with alcohol," Mama warns me, as she raises her eyebrows.

"I didn't know that, Mama. Thanks for letting me know."

"Linda's able to hear me a lot of the time," Aunt Ramona says wistfully. "I was able to get several of my ideas into *Cahas Mountain*. The part about Lakeside Amusement Park came from me. I used to love to go there. It's so funny when Linda thinks an idea comes from her but it's really from us. Maybe it's best we don't tell her *everything* now," Ramona says, teasing me. The others laugh.

"She always listened to you more than she did me while she was growing up," Mama chuckles. "You two were like kindred spirits. Oh, I see now that you really are! Often things get clearer from this vantage point, but not always. I didn't like how things were then, but I suppose now it's all right."

"Mama, where's Daddy," I ask, feeling emotions well up inside me. "Why isn't he here with you? I really miss him."

"Oh, this is girl time, and your dad's in the garden working, as usual. You know how he likes to grow things."

"Even where he is now? It seems to me he wouldn't have to work in a garden," I ask, full of concern.

"Your father is doing what he loves. At least now I don't have to honor that agreement I made with him that I would can or freeze anything he grew. That certainly was tiresome. Now I have all kinds of free time to do the things that I enjoy."

"Does that include spending time with me, dear sister?" Ramona asks with a sly grin. "If it does, we are making great progress

-153-

in our relationship. I agree with you that husbands can be difficult and are seldom worth the trouble. Not that they can't be fun from time to time."

"If you want your father to visit," Mama says, ignoring Ramona, and serving me a piece of pie, "I suggest you bring his collection of pipes downstairs. He always loved his pipes. You could probably light one up; I bet that would get his attention. Put on a football game. That will help too. And while you're getting his pipes, I want you to bring down my china doll and cradle. I'm feeling nostalgic."

"Don't forget my locket. I want to see the picture of Elbert and me on our wedding day," Grandmother says, "and don't forget the Bible."

"Bring down the gold pocket watch that belonged to your Uncle Dewey. You will find it in your father's desk," Mama says. "And please start wearing my opal ring. It's not doing any good in the bank's lock box," she adds as her eyes focus on my bare hand.

Grandmother rises from her chair and starts wiping down her kitchen table with Goddard's Wax Furniture Polish. "Now, it's time for you to go back to bed, Linda, and wake up in your world. We'll clean up, as usual, and be back next week."

"Thank you all for coming and for the apple pie," I say. "It was awfully nice of you all to show up in my kitchen. It was a very special surprise."

"Sweet dreams," Mama says. "I'll tell your father you said hello."

Grandmother, Mama, Aunt Ramona, and Mrs. Bernstein smile as I turn to climb the stairs.

Fiction

Womantis

LINDA KAY SIMMONS

My interest in writing has been interwoven with my life as a sky goddess. I have been on two spaceships in my 31 years of celestial adventures. The first spaceships were with Piedmont Airlines, the second USAirways. Commander Dick was a character I sometimes encountered in my earlier days of space travel.

"Yes, Betsy, it truly is a miraculous day here at the launch site at Bridgewater Plaza. The spaceship *Moon Quest* left Earth's orbit approximately twenty minutes ago. All systems checked out, and everything went smoothly. You could not ask for a better day. People are still rallying around here, and the people from the Crunchy-Munchy Cereal Company are ecstatic. They believe their investment in *Moon Quest* will more than pay off with all this publicity, not to mention the names of all their cereals painted on the outside of the spaceship."

"Hello, Larry. This is Betsy Jettison reporting from the new Naval Observatory in Moneta, Virginia. It certainly has been a wonderful day for the Observatory. Astronomers discovered in July of 2000 that the earth has a new neighbor. They accidently found what appears to be a tiny new moon orbiting Jupiter. Exploring this newly-discovered moon is what this space assignment is all about! Commander Dick Helms and his crew certainly seemed excited about this mission. This will be the farthest any of them have ever gone in interplanetary space. Imagine taking a mission to the smallest object orbiting any of the 8 planets in our solar system. The mission will take them fifty million miles from Jupiter!"

"Exactly, Betsy. This is why the people at Crunchy-Munchy Cereal Company believe their sales will orbit. No pun intended!

You also failed to mention that Alien Crunch Cereal is a complete food. There are marshmallow aliens in each box to satisfy any sweet tooth on board. This will be the only food for Commander Dick and his crew for one year. Their only beverage will be Crunchy-Munchy's Galaxy Space Water. It's great publicity for the Crunchy-Munchy Cereal Company, the United States, and the *Moon Quest Mission*.

'This is Larry Cyberson and Betsy Jettison signing off in Moneta, Virginia, for the Crunchy-Munchy Cereal Company's *Moon Quest program*. This has been live coverage from WSLK Broadcasting in Moneta, Virginia."

***

Commander Dick couldn't have been more pleased. The launch went better than planned. Things were just about perfect for him, except for having to eat that damned awful cereal for one year. Dick had always thought Teddy Howell was a great first officer and Max Lumpkin was O.K., even if he was a nerd. The team of space attendants was gorgeous. He was glad he insisted on picking his own crew. Hell, he knew there were better space attendants he could have chosen, especially the older ones. But he had to look at them for a whole year, and he wanted babes. *What can anyone expect*, he thought. *A guy's got to get laid. A year can be a really long time.*

Commander Dick began fantasizing. Ginny was his ideal space attendant. She was 5'9", tall and trim, and strong-arms-and-powerful-legs yummy. He liked how she played a little rough, too. Just the way he liked it. *Hell,* he thought, *I'll call her up now and tell her to bring me a bowl of that nasty cereal.* He made the call over the intercom, and it was only minutes before she arrived.

"Ginny, honey, you feeling O.K.? You're looking a little green. Is two weeks on this little old spaceship a bit much for you?"

"I'm all right. Here's your cereal. If you don't need me, I'll get back to my duties."

"Yeah, sure. But when you get through, come on up and visit me. The view is better when you're up here." He could have sworn that when he said this, he saw her head spin completely around.

"Shit, maybe I'm coming down with something," he said to Howell and Lumpkin.

They didn't reply. They never really listened when he tried to schmooze one of the girls. With Commander Dick, it was always the same old lines and routines.

"Hey, Howell, you and Lumpkin take charge for a while. I'm going to go lie down. I'm starting to see things."

When he awoke much later, he felt like he had been asleep for days.

"God, I feel bad. It feels like a thousand hands have been prodding my body. I must be really sick. Everything is fuzzy. I can't hear myself think," Commander Dick said to no one. He became woozy and lay down again. He slept for three days

.

***

Meanwhile, in the galley of the spaceship, newly-hatched praying mantises continued to eat their way out of the Alien Crunch Cereal boxes. It was easy to get out once hatched because of the sharp hooks on the arm-like legs. It took ten days for the entire larval mass to mature. The leaders had come out a few days earlier. They were larger, more slender winged insects than their comrades. All the new insects had to do was wait their turn, watch their leaders, and learn what to do next.

When the space attendants fell asleep, the next step of their journey began. The insects crawled upon the attendants' human forms and secreted their fluids on the bodies to paralyze them. Next, they worked their way inside the orifices, and claimed the attendants' bodies as their own, just as their leader had done. *Then they were womantises!*

***

'We have to secrete on him, in order to paralyze him. We can't take the chance of him waking up—at least for now," said Judy, the first womantis.

"It will be better when he is trained and we don't contaminate ourselves with our own fluids," said the second womantis.

"In an hour we will give him another secretion. Then we can propagate two of the new womantises while he is still unconscious. It would be better if he didn't wake up until they were impregnated and we are assured of the new life forms," said Judy, the first womantis who was clearly in charge.

"Do you mind if I go before the other two? I've never had a chance to go first," said womantis number two.

"Yes, but do hurry. We don't want to render him useless until we are through with the other two womantises," replied womantis number one.

***

Commander Dick awakened abruptly. *Hell, where are the others? Why hasn't anyone checked on me?* He could hardly focus. *Something odd has happened to me. Maybe I can make it to the control room if I hold on to something,* he thought.

"Howell, Lumpkin, where are you sons-of-bitches? What's going on?" He knew someone was there, he could sense them.

Someone or something grabbed him from behind. He kicked and attempted to lunge. He screamed but nothing came out. He fought as hard as he could, but something held him tight. He sensed they were female. He couldn't tell. He thought he could be having a nightmare, then everything faded from sight.

***

The womantises no longer bothered to inject Commander Dick. They were becoming cocky and confident in their human forms. One of the womantises had taken the body of 'His Beautiful Ginny.' She and one of the other womantises entered Commander Dick's room, naked except for the bottled water they held. 'His Beautiful Ginny' held the bottle to her lips, sipped, and then spoke.

"I am experiencing a different feeling for you, Commander Dick. My body no longer responds like it did the few times we copulated while human. In fact, you bore me."

"What do you mean, while human?" asked Commander Dick.

"I am not human. I am a womantis. All of your attendants are womantises, and we have taken over your spaceship," 'His Beautiful Ginny' answered, standing before him with her arms raised as if in prayer.

"What is this, a sick joke?" demanded the commander.

'His Beautiful Ginny' took the water bottle she had been sipping from and poured the contents over her ample green breast.

"Oh, God, Ginny, I'm so thirsty. Don't pour the water out like that. Give it to me!" the commander begged.

"I am no longer Ginny. I am womantis. Remember that. Now, Commander Dick, let us begin." 'His Beautiful Ginny' beckoned the other womantises to form a line to enter the commander's room.

He took a shallow breath. *God, help me keep my sanity*, he thought, as he willed his erection for the 32nd time.

When the womantises were through with him, he rose feebly and looked out into space. "My God, the ship is way off course. I must be looking at the two moons of Mars, Phobos and Deimos. Fear and Panic. How appropriate," he said, but there were no humans left to hear him. The commander dissolved onto the floor in hysterical laughter. It continued throughout the night.

***

"Good morning, Commander Dick. Here's a bit of Alien Crunch Cereal for you. You need to keep up your strength." 'His Beautiful Ginny' was back.

"What does it matter?" the commander replied curtly.

"Oh, it matters to us. Because of you, we will survive."

"What if I don't eat?"

"We will force you."

"What if you answer some questions for me, and I eat willingly?"

"We have always been willing to answer your questions, Commander Dick. All you need do is ask."

"Why have you done this? What have you done to Howell and Lumpkin? Where is the spaceship headed?"

"I might as well answer your questions and save myself and the others the trouble of being pestered by you each time one of us comes in for servicing. You people on Gaia call our planet Mars. We are the descendants of Ares. Our form, the womantis and manmantis, has lived on the moon of Mars known as Phobos for more than 3.6 billion years. Some of us have lived on Gaia. As you see, there has been much biological activity with our organic molecules and mineral features."

"How can this be? This is just mythology. How did you get to Earth?" asked the commander.

"We live in what you call the fourth and fifth dimensions. You and your kind have been trapped in your own world of length, width, and depth, and you have been oblivious to us. We have co-existed in a parallel universe. You could not see us because we have been "rolled" very small, to a size much smaller than a decimal point. But now our concept of space and time are breaking down. We can no longer sustain life because of inbreeding and having devoured all of our males. This is causing the deterioration of the Phobos orbit because it exists also in the fourth and fifth dimensions. We must get to Deimos or be destroyed. That is why we used the cereal on the spaceship as a means of escape."

"I don't understand," admitted the commander.

'His Beautiful Ginny' continued: "Ares' companion was Eris, the Greek goddess of discord and strife. She is jealous and sinister. Eris turned all females into praying mantises. In this form she felt we would always be in homage to her and Ares would never be tempted by our beauty. She cursed us by allowing the females to live only on the flesh of our males. Most of us now live on the body of our father, Mars, with almost no ability to reproduce. In 50 million years, if we are not extinct, Phobos will crash onto the surface of Mars. A cruel joke. That is why we need to relocate to Deimos."

"So, that is why you took over the spaceship?" asked the commander.

"Yes, because in the future, humans will be on Deimos using it as a space station. This will be our salvation. By propagating with you now, in our Gaia bodies, we will have enough Gaia characteristics to sustain us, until humans create the space station."

***

The creature Ginny had left him a half bottle of Galaxy Water and a box of Alien Crunch Cereal. He had not had water in over twenty-four hours or eaten for forty-eight. He guzzled the water in one deep drink and then scooped out big handfuls of cereal. It was then he felt something move. He looked closer and saw some things that looked like eggs or larva.

"Damn bitches, they've given me maggots to eat," he cried out.

He emptied the box on the floor and retrieved a microscope from his desk. Baby praying mantises were hatching and crawling about.

"They all have my face on their praying mantis bodies!" he screamed in horror.

From outside he heard the womantises laughing. *This is what the mating experiences were all about*, he thought. Commander Dick knew all eyes were watching; there were four state-of-the-art cameras aimed right at him.

***

That night he heard two of the womantises talking.

"We have assumed there may be a use for this human, but after observing him, is there really? We have taken all the fluids we need from Commander Dick. I suggest we eat him now," said a womantis with an impatient tone.

He recognized Ginny's voice: "You might be right, but we still have a few more days before we land to decide what to do with him."

"We don't have to decide now. Besides, we still have plenty of meat left from the other two," replied one of the other womantis space attendants.

Oh my God, that's what happened to Howell and Lumpkin. These creatures are cannibals! I will not, I cannot, panic. I must stay cool. I have to bide my time and devise a plan. I will plead with them to let me live until I have impregnated them all! I am so weak I must eat. The commander tried to think rationally as hundreds of thoughts were pouring into his head.

He forced himself to pick out and eat the flakes scattered around the small creatures, which covered the floor. He tried not to see his own face in the green insects, looking back at him at least a thousand times over.

***

He stared out of the spaceship for days, trying to convince himself that he was delusional. More than once he was sure his heart had stopped. The moon Deimos looked lifeless. This far out he could see no vegetation. This new world was coming closer. Yet, the nearer it came to him, the more it seemed to fade away. The pale colors seemed unable to form anything solid.

Finally the spaceship landed on the womantises' asteroid moon, Phobos. No sooner had the door opened than the commander heard the battle cry of one of the womantises.

"We should eat him now. We have no more use for him. Let us feast on male human meat and celebrate!"

Then something happened which completely altered his state of mind.

The small child-mantises seemed to know that he was their human "father." They instantly and completely covered his body, creating an armor.

"Mothers, you will have to kill each of us if you try to harm our father. By harming us, you will in turn destroy our asteroid world," the children all chanted together.

The commander, as if in sudden inspiration, yelled out: "These small creatures are half-human! They have feelings for me. Because of this, I will willingly stay on your planet and cooperate with saving your asteroid-moon culture. I have a new feeling, one of deep affection for my small protégés."

Commander Dick knew he could never find his way back to Earth without Howell and Lumpkin, but this he would never say. Besides, it felt good the way the child-mantises looked up to and prayed to him. As they saw it, he alone saved their moon. The child-mantises in turn could keep him from being devoured. The thought came to him that maybe he could even get something going with his 'His Beautiful Ginny' again.

***

Many years later, humans arrived on Deimos to establish the base that had been predicted. The womantises kept a close eye on the construction of the space station on their moon.

Still they waited, days, weeks, years for the space station to be completed.

Then, one wondrous day, they decided they no longer needed Commander Dick. The space station was functional, and the first of many great spaceships had docked.

'His Beautiful Ginny' watched in awe as the first great ship nosed in to the station, her hull sparkling and new. Her name was painted on the side: *Moneta*. Ginny smiled. The waiting was over. On that very day, the womantises made the old man, Commander Dick, their prey. It was a day of feasting and celebrating. The time of the womantis had come!

Poetry

Through Roseveare's Glasses

MELISSA "MJ" STEPHENS

This—a tribute to fame.
You see,
a tumor got her brain.
Life never the same,
Just more wind and rain.

These are Roseveare's glasses,
I'm just lookin' through her glasses,
—her glasses, Roseveare's glasses.

A wicked eye so soft,
Vivid images present.
The high limbs—lofted,
a window's angle bent.

The colorful lens of her glasses,
Roseveare's glasses—her glasses.

All challenges are set,
the detective does solve,
a scene where crosses met,
neither rosey, red nor mauve.

Through her glasses,
Roseveare's glasses,
Teaching us all—through glasses.

That soul of grace.
Toughness—must embrace,
But, in a happier place,
A character of time—
And space.

Poetry

The Opposites

MELISSA "MJ" STEPHENS

You are right-handed, I am left,
you are bold and brimming, I am shy and reserved,
you have a dog, I, a cat,
you enjoy cocktails and wine, I, a beer or bourbon,
you and your leather, I and my wool,
you thrive in cities, I amid rivers and trees.

We are a microcosm—don't you see?

You scoff at sport, I rely upon a game,
you and your fedora, I with my ski rag,
you enjoy the club scene, I the quiet houses of theatre,
you and your cigarettes, my lack of interest in the vice,
you are single with grown children, I am married with some, too.

A near polarity—does it bother you?

You are persistent, I am patient,
you have style and color, I, in my muted tones and hues,
you enjoy the beats, I savor the blues,
you and your cappuccino, I with my tea.

How is it at all—you and I can agree?

Poetry

Tennessee '49

MELISSA MJ" STEPHENS

I woke one evening;
Walked along gravel to find sustenance.
There were two—with guitars.

Wondering about Tennessee.

I feasted on pork and jambalaya;
We are just temporaries of time and place.
One started to play—the other nodded.

I listened to them harmonize;
Finishing my kale and tea.
Two fiddles arrived—women this time.

Singing about ol' Tennessee.

I heard all the sounds meld;
A simple impromptu for nobody.
The quad finished—and bid adieu.

I thanked them for the gift;
Awake and forever remembering.
A sweet summer moment—in Virginia.

Thinking about Tennessee '49.

Nonfiction

How to Name a Dog

MARK YOUNG

There are three main approaches to naming a dog. The first, highly recommended by dog trainers, dog psychologists, and the like, is to name your dog with a short, crisp moniker in order quickly to gain the attention of the dog, showing your superior alpha relationship.

My parents did just that with our first dog, a highly-trained, obedient English Welsh Terrier named Crip. Notice that the name when spoken in a raised commanding voice almost sounds like a bark, guaranteeing the dog will pay attention to whatever command follows the call.

Well, to tell the truth, that kind of naming gets boring. But I am getting ahead of myself.

About a year after Crip died, winning the psychological battle between parent and child over a new dog became our quest. We had to have another dog. And as it turned out, a year of nagging was long enough for us to bring our parents close to the edge of insanity. Each night we carefully brought them just a little closer to the tipping point, until finally they gave in.

To this day, I can still see that famous vision of Lassie the wonder dog running through a field. That vision had etched itself on the insides of my eyelids., and it may have been the only thing my two siblings and I willingly shared. But share we did. And so we plotted.

Over that year, we developed what we thought was the near-perfect logic. We swore that we would do all the doggy chores, learn the responsibilities of pet ownership, and be closer siblings. We swore it would make us a more loving family. All this and more would be possible if only we had a dog.

We would learn to be better Christians, take better care of the environment, be better citizens, be examples for all of Christendom. We would grow up to be doctors, lawyers and scientists, be all the things they wanted us to be. Wait, there's more! Maybe even win an Olympic medal or two. Or a Nobel Prize! Why not?

We swore we would take care of our parents in their old age. All it would take for this miracle transformation to happen was for us to become proud owners of a dog. It was clear that we needed a dog to help guide us into adulthood.

I faulted my parents for not knowing better. I trusted them not to trust us, but they did. It must be in the best interest of the species for parents to see their children through some sort of rose-colored veil, to see only the charitable goodness and kindness in them. Or maybe it was just because it was the fifties. Optimism ran rampant, as abundant as wildflowers after a spring rain.

Then one glorious night, as we sat around the dining room table, our parents proclaimed in a joint parental decree that they'd had an epiphany. And behold, a light entered the room and shone upon them as they announced that having another dog would be an opportunity for us to understand the responsibilities of adulthood, to learn the value of work.

I looked at my older brother. From his expression I knew we shared the same thought, "You have got to be kidding. Is this the best they can come up with after all our efforts?" After all, we'd just put in a full year of dog propaganda. I shrugged. Oh well. Wait a minute—I forgot what was important: WE WERE GETTING A DOG!!

Not only were we getting a dog, but we were getting to name it. My father droned on about the responsibilities of owning a dog. We had to decide who was going to do what and something about something, and something about some other thing and something about something else. I was only thinking, *We are getting a dog, and we have to make sure the name of the dog is cool.*

Which brings me to the second category of ways to name a dog. This involves choosing a name that is REALLY COOL.

As soon as dinner was over, the now-three amigos raced into the living room. At that very moment my parents, watching my brother, sister, and me work together for the first time in their lives, were as proud of us as they had ever been or, for that matter, ever would be.

How fleeting the joys of parenthood.

We kicked around all the standard names and quite a few odd ones, but nothing was cool enough or different enough to stand out. Then my brother came up with one that fit all three of our demented imaginations. It was perfect, philosophical yet simple. We would call the dog "I Am."

It was a proud statement of being one with the universe. And at that very moment we quietly, unknowingly slipped into the sixties, into the Age of Aquarius.

But back to the task at hand. We had a first name, but we had to have a last name that would be of equal significance and importance. I said, "I got it. 'Ono'. 'I AM ONO,' as in 'I am, oh no, (a dog).'"

Metaphysically perfect. We had no idea how precocious we were. Or for that matter, what metaphysically meant, but who cared? What mattered was we had a cool name. It dawned on me as we savored the results of our "naming meeting that it carried an unexpected, potentially hilarious bonus.

"Can't you see Mom out in the middle of the front yard yelling for the dog to come in, 'Here I am. Here I am.'"

My brother rolled on the floor laughing.

I warned. "We can't tell them."

My parents were not thrilled with the name we had chosen, but true to their word, they let it stand. They failed to realize, as most of us who are parents do not realize, the unintended consequences of parental approval.

Within the year, my mother was out in the yard most every night calling out to the universe through the eternal darkness, "Here I Am, here I Am." It still never fails to bring a smile.

We had several dogs after I Am, but for some reason they all came pre-named.

The third approach to naming a dog is using those names that are ironic or are double entendres. This approach is far and away my favorite, one I was not able to implement until I was grown and married. I had a crazed English Setter bent on hunting anything down, killing anything that moved. We named it "Pax Romana" after the two hundred years of world peace during the days of the Roman Empire. A mean-looking Rhodesian Ridgeback, a breed originally bred to hunt lions, we named Mokey, after the female hare-brained artist philosopher in a Muppet show.

My favorite was a name with a secret family meaning. We got a cockapoo, which happens to be a little frou frou of a dog, as a Christmas present for our kids some thirty years after I Am died. We were forced to come up with a fitting name for that oversized gerbil. My initial favorites were Thor, Cyclops or maybe Frankenstein. My wife rejected those out of hand.

"Okay, How about Troll, or Ghoul, or Medusa?"

"The kids will want to name her Snow Ball, or Fluffy, or Muffy, or Fuzz."

I told her I was putting my foot down. I puffed out my chest.

"If we have to have a frou frou dog, it is not going to have a frou frou name."

Most of the time she let me think I was king. But once again, I am getting ahead of my story.

My part of the story starts with my realization that my mother-in-law and I were not the best of friends. I was sure from her perspective she believed my wife could have done much better than marrying me. My wife, on the other hand, assured me I just intimidated her. I knew better. Her mother and I knew exactly what we thought of each other.

Anyway, my mother-in-law had a way of making me disappear even when I was in the same room. I could be standing three feet away from her. She would say something like, "What is he doing now?" or "When is he going?" or "Where is he?" The woman seldom acknowledged my existence, never called me by name. At one point, after we had been married for over a decade, I stood up, walked over to her, and reintroduced myself to her saying, "Hello, my name is Mark. I am happy to meet you. Feel free to call me by my first name anytime you like."

Diplomacy wasn't my strong suit, but what the heck. I tried the "peace in our time" approach. It didn't work for Chamberlain. It didn't work for me.

I began to refer to my mother-in-law as Grendel. For those who are uninitiated, Grendel was the first monster in English literature. It just seemed to fit her.

Apparently, at a party one New Year's Eve that I only vaguely remember, I made an off-handed reference to her by that nickname. With a little encouragement from my fellow partiers and under the influence of, well, something, I suddenly was acting out how she, beginning from her lair in Florida, waiting for the last half of the blackest of nights, made her way north. Hidden under this veil of darkness, taking nourishment only from the moss that grows on the north side of trees, she began her journey north until, tree by tree, night by night, state by state, she found us in the most northern region of New York State.

As the kids got older, my wife worried they would find out we weren't really that fond of discussing the finer points of *Beowulf*, and in an act of self-defense she named the little cockapoo we got for Christmas Grendel. Whether she named it after her mother or the first monster in English literature I will leave to your imagination. I prefer to think of it as just a happy coincidence.

For her part, my mother-in-law never understood how we could name such a pretty little dog Grendel. She would never call the dog anything but Gretchen. For my part, I never ceased to enjoy throwing the ball for Grendel to fetch and bring it back to me, obediently dropping it at my feet.

Fiction

The Interlocking Rings

MARK YOUNG

With his eyes on the floor of the amphitheater, Dr. Richard Abrams paces in front of the idealistic college students, aware that he lives for these performances, his own personal "Shakespearean" moment.

He silently paraphrases the Bard, *To strut and fret upon the stage until I'm heard no more.*

He follows the cracks across the cement floor, being careful not to step on them.

He visualizes a small group of intercity girls skipping along the dirty city sidewalk, *Step on a crack, break my mother's back, step on a line, break my father's spine.* He grimaces as he fails to miss the final crack.

The students squirm and jabber in the small amphitheater seats neatly lined up in elevated stadium rows before him. With an unexpected flourish, he shakes the image of the little girls from his consciousness, turns, and slowly raises his head as if he were raising an invisible curtain. He faces the upperclassmen. His eyes find the middle of the auditorium and, with his glare, he intimidates them into silent submission.

***

A few hours earlier his friend and colleague, a young psychology professor, joins him at a Starbucks just off campus.

After the usual greeting rituals Richard asks, "What have you been up to?"

"Finishing up a paper tracing the history of some of the more popular childhood superstitions. It's quite impressive how the unconscious mind works." He takes a sip of coffee.

"You know that little ditty about stepping on a crack? It turns out to be grounded in black magic or, depending on subculture, a spell used to release evil trapped in the underground. Its common usage dates back to the early 1800s. I've found references dating back even farther to African slave religions. Interesting, isn't it—the notion that stepping on a crack can curse the future? What about you?"

Richard tells him about a new computer game he installed the night before and the enjoyment he has taking down the CGI (Computer-Generated Imagery) enemies. He uses computer games to kill the boredom that settled in after his divorce—computer games and now a new love interest he doesn't want to discuss with his friend. He keeps the conversation focused on the CGIs.

"Attacking the CGI enemies is like finding the unprepared students in my lectures."

His friend says, "Don't make teaching sound like a computer game."

"Are you sure it isn't? Because I think that's what we do, destroy the pious, the naïve, the pseudo-intellectuals, and the self-indulgent upperclassmen with the guns of our superior intellect." Richard raises his coffee cup and offers a toast, "To another day of enlightening the ignorant. It is, after all, our life's mission, isn't it?"

"You're depressing me." His colleague lifts his coffee cup in return. "But yes, I guess it is, as long as you realize you're only replacing the power of the joystick with..."

Richard holds his hand up and interrupts, "You're not going 'Freudian' on me, are you?"

His colleague laughs. "I was talking about a game console, but, if a Freudian image works for you, so much the better. As I was saying, if all you're doing is replacing the power of the joystick with a list of titles ending with Ph.D., then cloaking yourself in intellectualism is being more bully than teacher."

***

A small distraction brings Dr. Abrams back to the present. He allows himself a half-smile as he stands in front of the students. He doesn't think of himself as a bully, and yet, if he is honest, he's not entirely uncomfortable with the title. For the first time, he allows himself to survey the hundred or so upperclassmen stuffed into the lecture hall. He speaks across the small microphone attached to his collar. "Today we will address two contemporary myths.

"The most significant myth of our time is that somehow, between the onslaught of technology and the age of communication, we control the planet's future. In reality, it is and always has been the planet that controls ours.

"We've come to believe that with our political and economic greatness comes the power to control world history. And not merely the history of humankind, but because we have convinced ourselves that we are responsible for climate change, we've convinced ourselves that we can control nature as well. This myth may have originated from our ability to control the small micro-climate in our homes and workplaces. From there we've also convinced ourselves we can control nature's macro-climate as well."

A voice comes from the auditorium. "Dr. Abrams, do you not believe in the science of climate change?"

He looks down at his seating chart to cover up the fact that he is well aware of who is speaking. He pushes back the image of her naked body. "Emily, what I believe is not the point. My point and my question are one in the same." He raises his head to address the group. "What have you done to question what you believe? Have you researched and analyzed the sources of your beliefs, or just allowed yourselves to be fed the pabulum of the current political class in power?"

A voice comes from the back section of the auditorium "But, Professor, the research is done. Why waste time? Get on with fixing the problem before it's too late."

Dr. Abrams walks behind the lectern in front of the lecture

hall, once again checks the seating chart. "Rich, correct?"

"Yes, sir."

He addresses the hall, "Listen to yourselves as you defend theories on rising ocean levels that are not rising above the margin of error, the catastrophe of melting ice fields as if they have never melted before, CO_2 projections based on historically-biased entry data points.

"Have you not been taught that generations of our ancestors fell prey to the same arrogance? That of creating scientific thought, or 'truths' as some of you are fond of calling then, from limited observations? Take a moment to consider these other, at the time, untestable theories. Ones that were solely based on man's myopic observation—the world is flat, pregnancy comes from sleeping with the window open, marijuana is the gateway to addiction, or AIDS is 'God's curse' on sexual sinners. I ask you, what common root do all of these share?"

He dramatically waits for an answer, knowing there won't be one. He clears his throat. "It is quite simple."

He raises his voice. "It's the power-seeker's ability to create fear. And that done, open the opportunity for persons seeking power and money to fix what in reality is unbroken. When have the predictions of global starvation ever materialized, or world overpopulation threatened world civilization?"

He pauses. "Here is your lesson for today. Write it down. You will see it again and again. Follow the trail of money the doomsayers create and ignore their predictions. One would have done well to invest in multinational food conglomerates. The pharmaceutical companies that developed cures and the pharmacies that distributed them. Or companies that invested in ethanol and the manufacturers of wind power turbines and lithium batteries. As long as there is public fear, the government won't allow companies that claim to provide a solution to fail. It will subsidize them into profitability. They have learned this lesson well, 'Necessity is the mother of invention,' and so they have invented the necessity and financed the invention."

He ignores the mumblings rippling through what now have

become the uncomfortable stadium seats. "If you want to understand social history, you must also understand this. It is the second most prevalent social myth out there today—the myth that societies change because of group action. Social history teaches us that social change and behavior are not produced by groups but by the actions of lone individuals, persons who stand apart and ignore the fears produced by the moneychangers. Single fish in a school of fish that suddenly change direction, and the entire school follows."

"Dr. Abrams, now are you rejecting the concept of group consensus?"

He refers once more to his seating chart. "David, it is not the herd that makes a difference; it merely repeats the current mantra. It is the single individual that stands against it. It is the man or woman who denies the arguments of the apologists, who rejects the fear of standing alone.

"Don't confuse it with whether or not the change is for the better or worse for that society. That is an entirely different argument that is best left to the historians to decipher.

"I'm sure you can give me example after example of these single individuals. Whether it be Columbus or Hitler, Julius Caesar or George Washington, Jesus or Mohammed. If you think those are to whom I refer, you are missing the point. Each of us has within us the power to be that single fish.

"Let me tell you the story of such an ordinary person. A person like you and me, a man history forgets, but not the reforms he caused to have happened. The planet created the potato famine that swept Ireland and depleted the population of that country by some twenty-five percent, ravaged them through starvation and emigration.

"One such emigrant was swept up from Ireland and deposited on the streets of the Philadelphia Harbor, a politically-corrupt city where thousands of "Ulstermen" entered the United States. On the evening of the elections of 1868, he was a member of the Philadelphia police force. Listed as a common laborer at first, he moved up in his new life, maybe as far as his heritage would allow in that so-called City of Brotherly Love. The afternoon of the election, at the request of the neighbors in the precinct, he was assigned to help protect the ballot box.

"The polls were about to close as he watched an unruly group of men approach the voting booth for the third time. It was not uncommon for political social club members to grow their beards and mustaches, vote once, then shave their beards and vote again, and finally, clean-shaven, cast their third ballot.

"The unruly men turn into a mob of more than a hundred. Shots are fired. The outer ring of the police officers guarding the polls breaks down. They flee like a scared school of baitfish. Unaware they have left, this one officer is soon surrounded by the mob. The officer holds one of the rioters and attempts to arrest him. A third man slips up behind him and strikes him on the back of the head with a blackjack. He fights off these men, and in the struggle, he is shot in the upper lip. The ball struck his teeth, is deflected and passes out through the lips, tearing a portion of his nose; his right eye turns black. More shots. He takes a ball in the foot. He breaks away from the men and makes his way across the street to a tavern.

"He warns the others inside to get upstairs, out of the way. They quickly take his advice; he follows a few steps, then turns and limps back down the stairs. He takes out his pistol and looks at it. At that moment, he makes a fatal choice of duty and honor above everything else.

"The school of fish is about to change direction.

"He hobbles out the door and onto the street, blood running down his face. Again he is shot. The ball enters his back, three inches to the left of his spinal column; the ball passes beneath the eleventh rib, through the spleen and diaphragm, through the upper part of the stomach and the left lung. He hemorrhages. He drops to the ground. Three hours later he dies.

"The school of fish turns.

"The election process changes and the corruption that plagued the city heals itself. Not since then has a policeman ever been killed in a national election.

"History, my young intellectuals, tells us to arm ourselves against the evils of the mob."

***

Emily sits on the twin bed in the dormitory, slowly looking around at Mick's room, wondering how long it would take him to come back with food from the snack room in the dorm basement.

Impatience is her downfall, impatience and curiosity. It is not that she is unaware of it. She lists them as major faults on her personality profile. She knows they are the most significant contributors to her troubles, going back farther than she can remember.

It's those evil twins that have created a series of unfortunate decisions ending in her current relationship with Mick and causing her present predicament. It is curiosity over a relationship with an older man that got her involved with Dr. Richard Abrams in the first place, a man with more experience than the boys she's been dating. Someone whom she hopes might awaken the emotions she reads about in the coming-of-age novels she loves. She is impatient for that awaking. So far, the results from boys in her age group had been disappointing.

She gets up and stretches her legs, wanders over to Mick's desk. It's a contrast to hers. He's the opposite of everything she is, which is one of the things that attracted her to him in the first place.

His desk is piled high with papers with no discernable logic. She can't resist straightening them, at first just stacking them neatly. Then she begins separating them based on their subject matter; civil disobedience and revolutions, chemistry, and diagramed electrical connections. These last seem particularly strange to her because she isn't aware he has any interest in engineering. As far as she knows sociological theory is as scientific as he gets. She runs her fingers over the spines of the books that lie open as she reads the titles, books on social evolution, commentaries on a corrupt society, the plight of the poor white working class, the coming environmental destruction of the earth, and the corruption of the money state. A shiver runs through her. She reacts by trying to return the pile of papers to their original disorganized groupings. She's now sure she is going to break things off with him.

What at first was an intriguing coupling has become increasingly worrisome. She knows what originally attracted her to him. She liked the fact that she was in charge, the decision maker, the dominant player. That is until Richard showed an interest in her and she began to experience the part of the seductress. It wasn't long until she enjoyed playing that role much more.

Shaking, she returns to the bed and begins remaking it, using the hospital corners her mother taught her. Her hand hits something buried beneath the mattress. She pulls out a notebook from under the sheets. In large block letters, the word *Manifesto* stares back at her. The air leaves her lungs as if she's been hit by a punch. Frightened, she spins and sits on the bed. Sweat forms on her upper lip as she reads.

Mick opens the door balancing a small pizza box and a couple of cans of soda in one hand. She is so focused on his notes she doesn't hear him enter until he speaks.

"What are you doing?"

She jumps at the sound of his voice, turns, faces him, puts the notebook behind her. Finding her nerve, she shoves it towards him and asks, "What's this?"

Mick is silent as he tries to control the quivering that is running through his body. Almost in slow motion, he puts the pizza and sodas on the bed and takes the notebook away from Emily. His silence frightens her. Regaining his composure, he whispers. "What do you think it is?"

Emily cringes, afraid to say what she's thinking. "I asked you first."

He tenses again, fighting back the need to strike out. He forces a smile, "It's just a private blog, you know, like a journal only more to the point. Don't worry about it, let's eat." He searches her eyes, then looks away. "How much did you read?"

She doesn't move."Why is Dr. Abrams' name listed and then scratched out?"

His anger flares, "Are you going to pretend you don't know?

How much did you read?"

She turns red. He couldn't possibly know about them. She was pretty sure no one knew. The relationship is too new for gossip, and they both have been cautious. She hasn't told anyone. Not even her best friend and roommate. She was sure Richard hasn't said anything. It is still too casual, not even worthy of a footnote, at least not yet. She turns defensive and says, "Know what?"

"Come on. Don't play stupid."

She holds her breath.

He begins again, "You know Abrams is one of them, one of the worst of them, for that matter."

She exhales in relief. Maybe Mick doesn't know. She tries to divert him. "I don't get it, one of what?"

"The radical anti-progressives. They're destroying the planet, Sitting around denying global warming, building walls to protect their race and religion's self-serving superiority, stepping on the less fortunate, believing the only lives that matter are theirs just so they can live better at the expense of our generation. He's a parasite living off the tuition money we pour into this place and not giving a damn how he and his group of cronies are destroying the world or how much we sacrifice to pay the debts we have to shoulder just to get brainwashed.

"Agree and get an 'A.' Tell the truth and fail. As long as he eats steak, the rest of the world can eat crap and wear masks to protect against the pollution they've created."

"But why is his name crossed out?" she asks.

He doesn't answer at first, then, "I don't know. I just don't like him. Why are you so fixated on him?"

"It just seems weird."

Anger wells up from the pit of his stomach, "Forget about it. Do you want pizza or not?"

"I guess." She takes the pizza box to the desk, and with her hand shoves the papers to one side so that he won't know she was snooping.

"Mick, we have to talk. I think we should stop seeing each other."

He doesn't say anything. Rage races across his face.

Emily's eyes widen.

"Oh, shit," she says, realizing how much more he has invested in their relationship than she does.

He spits out, "You can't be serious. You're dropping me because of a journal entry?"

"No, it's not that. Answer me, why do you have his name crossed out?"

"Why do you care so much about him? He's just a pompous ass."

"I've never seen this side of you. I thought I knew you better, that's all." She tries for a graceful exit, stumbling for words. "Maybe it's just I'm not political. Our partying has all been just fun, right? I mean 'no harm, no foul,' right? Just fun and games, right?"

"You'll be better off if you don't cross me."

There was no mistaking the menace in his voice.

She tenses. "Don't be angry; it's not like we won't be friends. Just think of us like a meteor in the night sky—we just burnt out crossing the darkness, that's all."

"You're sleeping with him, aren't you?"

"No, of course not."

"Don't cross me."

"What do you mean?"

"You're lying, and you're not very good at it."

"How can you say that?"

"I followed you."

***

The doors of the back of the amphitheater burst open and slam against the wall, announcing his presence in the lecture hall. Pieces of drywall fall from the cracks and onto the floor.

Dr. Abrams can say only "shit" into the sound system. He recognizes Mick from the practice range. They often pass each other there. The first time it left Dr. Abrams with an uncanny feeling that they had met somewhere before. He passed it off as one of those deja vu moments everyone has and thinks nothing more about it.

Mick raises his AR-15-style rifle modified to use a magazine that can hold a hundred bullets and waits for the student body to turn and face him. He views Emily through the sight and waits for her to recognize him, then puts a bullet through her head. Brain matter and pieces of her skull rain down on her friends. Her nearly headless body falls backward. Students panic, scream. He swings the rifle towards Abrams and fires several rounds before he turns it on those who run towards the front exits. There he mows them down as others dive under their seats. The deafening sound fills the theater.

Mick's first bullet enters Abram's upper lip. It strikes his teeth, is deflected, and passes out through the lips, tearing a portion of his nose; his right eye turns black. He grabs the lectern for support. He reaches down and draws the revolver from his ankle holster. He rests his arm on the lectern, aims at Mick with his uninjured eye, and fires one shot and then another and another. Mick's eyes widen as he realizes he's shot.

Abrams spins away from the lectern and is hit again. He takes a bullet in the foot. As Mick fires his last rounds at him, he falls to the ground and dies as the last bullet he fires enters Abrams' back, three inches to the left of his spinal column. The bullet passes beneath the eleventh rib, through the spleen and diaphragm, through the upper part of the stomach and the left lung. He hemorrhages. He drops to the ground. Three hours later he is dead.

***

"Welcome, welcome, welcome. I'm sure everything is a bit confusing at this point, but as you get acclimated, you'll remember all the challenges you've forgotten. Don't be alarmed if it isn't just the recent ones. You may also recall others from your various other journeys.

"It will be easier if you let yourself relax. As you get more comfortable, you will become aware of the repetition of a great many of these challenges. Each time you reacted to one, you were scored on how you handled it. Most often on a pass-or-fail basis based on your most current morality profile. Of course, you'll be given an opportunity to improve on these decisions during your next set of challenges. Your guides will review them with you and be as helpful as they can. After some time, when you are comfortable and ready, you may ask for what we kindly call a redo. We will arrange a new life for you to try again. Until that time we will use the latest name you are familiar with to make the adjustment as comfortable as possible. Now you'll meet with your guides for further, as you like to say in your lifespan, 'debriefing.'"

A guide contacts Richard Abrams. "You have a lot of questions. We find it easier if you wait to ask them. It's less of a shock. All will become clear before you start your redo."

"May I ask one question?"

"Of course. We are here to help you progress upward along the interlocking rings."

"What about the shooter and Emily?"

"You three have quite the repetitive history of love triangles. I can show you if you like."

"Please."

"What period of human history would you like to begin with?"